Books

Historical Western Romance Series

Redemption Mountain

Redemption's Edge, Book One
Wildfire Creek, Book Two
Sunrise Ridge, Book Three
Dixie Moon, Book Four
Survivor Pass, Book Five
Promise Trail, Book Six
Deep River, Book Seven
Courage Canyon, Book Eight
Forsaken Falls, Book Nine
Solitude Gorge, Book Ten
Rogue Rapids, Book Eleven
Angel Peak, Book Twelve
Restless Wind, Book Thirteen
Storm Summit, Book Fourteen
Mystery Mesa, Book Fifteen
Thunder Valley, Book Sixteen
A Very Splendor Christmas, Holiday Novella, Book Seventeen
Paradise Point, Book Eighteen,
Silent Sunset, Book Nineteen
Rocky Basin, Book Twenty, Coming Next in the Series!

MacLarens of Boundary Mountain

Colin's Quest, Book One,

Brodie's Gamble, Book Two
Quinn's Honor, Book Three
Sam's Legacy, Book Four
Heather's Choice, Book Five
Nate's Destiny, Book Six
Blaine's Wager, Book Seven
Fletcher's Pride, Book Eight
Bay's Desire, Book Nine
Cam's Hope, Book Ten

MacLarens of Fire Mountain

Tougher than the Rest, Book One
Faster than the Rest, Book Two
Harder than the Rest, Book Three
Stronger than the Rest, Book Four
Deadlier than the Rest, Book Five
Wilder than the Rest, Book Six

Romantic Suspense

Eternal Brethren, Military Romantic Suspense

Steadfast, Book One
Shattered, Book Two
Haunted, Book Three
Untamed, Book Four
Devoted, Book Five
Faithful, Book Six
Exposed, Book Seven
Undaunted, Book Eight
Resolute, Book Nine

Unspoken, Book Ten
Defiant, Book Eleven, Coming Next in the Series!

Peregrine Bay, Romantic Suspense

Reclaiming Love, Book One
Our Kind of Love, Book Two
Edge of Love, Book Three, Coming Next in the Series!

Contemporary Romance Series

MacLarens of Fire Mountain

Second Summer, Book One
Hard Landing, Book Two
One More Day, Book Three
All Your Nights, Book Four
Always Love You, Book Five
Hearts Don't Lie, Book Six
No Getting Over You, Book Seven
'Til the Sun Comes Up, Book Eight
Foolish Heart, Book Nine

Macklin's of Burnt River

Thorn's Journey
Del's Choice
Boone's Surrender

The best way to stay in touch is to subscribe to my newsletter. Go to: https://www.shirleendavies.com/ and subscribe in the box at the top of the right column that asks for your email. You'll be notified of new books before they are released, have chances to win great prizes, and receive other subscriber-only specials.

Silent Sunset

Redemption Mountain Historical Western Romance Series

SHIRLEEN DAVIES

Book Nineteen in the Redemption Mountain
Historical Western Romance Series

Copyright © 2021 by Shirleen Davies

All rights reserved. No part of this publication may be reproduced, distributed, or transmitted in any form or by any electronic or mechanical means, including information storage and retrieval systems or transmitted in any form or by any means without the prior written permission of the publisher, except by a reviewer who may quote brief passages in a review. Thank you for respecting the hard work of this author.

For permission requests, contact the publisher.

Avalanche Ranch Press, LLC
PO Box 12618
Prescott, AZ 86304

Silent Sunset is a work of fiction. Names, characters, places, and incidents are either products of the author's imagination or used fictitiously. Any resemblance to actual events, locales, or persons, living or dead, is wholly coincidental.

Book design and conversions by Joseph Murray at 3rdplanetpublishing.com

Cover design by Jaycee DeLorenzo at Sweet 'N Spicy Designs

ISBN: 978-1-947680-49-4

I care about quality, so if you find an error, please contact me via email at
shirleen@shirleendavies.com

Description

They took her life and forever love.
It's time to take them back.

Shane Banderas is ready to move on with his life. As a deputy in Splendor, a town he'd grown to love, the time had come to buy a place, marry, and start a family. Six years had passed since losing the only woman he'd ever loved. Years he'd never get back. Time to live for the present, and with luck, a new kind of future.

Angela Baldwin refuses to live under the strict standards of Boston society. Ready to break away, she and her close friend head west toward the love stolen from her six long years before. Refusing to consider he may have already married another, she boards the train. She has little going for her except a determination to win him back.

Shane can't believe what is right in front of him. Angie, the woman who'd left him years ago, is standing on the boardwalk, as if she belongs there. He knew the truth about her. Trust isn't a word she understands.

With no desire to rekindle feelings for an old love, he continues his plans to court another. A beautiful woman with a sharp mind and quick wit. A woman he can trust and share a future.

Endangering any future is the threat of an old adversary seeking vengeance for a perceived wrong. An outlaw who enjoys killing, including those close to his prey. Everyone important to Shane.

Silent Sunset, book nineteen in the Redemption Mountain historical western romance series, is a novel with an HEA and no cliffhanger.

Visit my website for a list of characters for each series.
http://www.shirleendavies.com/character-list.html

Silent Sunset

Chapter One

Splendor Montana
Summer 1872

"You don't have to die today." Deputy Shane Banderas's unflinching voice echoed through the almost empty street.

"I'm not expecting to." The brawny cowboy's hand hovered over the butt of his six-shooter, his slurred words indicating the inaccurate claim.

Shane had watched the card game inside the Wild Rose for an hour while sipping a single pour of whiskey. During the same time, the cowboy had consumed half a bottle while his winnings declined. He'd poured another finger with each loss, until his agitation exploded.

"You drew your gun on one of the men at your table. Can't have that in Splendor." Shane adjusted his stance, positioning himself for the shot he hoped didn't happen.

"He was cheating," the cowboy growled, glancing at the men on the boardwalk.

"So you said. There's a problem, though."

"What's that?" Swaying, the cowboy widened his booted feet, almost toppling over.

"No one else agreed with you. Can't have you kill a man over a misunderstanding." Shane spotted fellow deputy, Hawke DeBell, move a few feet behind the drunk.

"Tell you what, drop the gunbelt and we'll give you the best bed in jail."

The man guffawed, scratching the back of his neck. "I ain't staying in no jail."

"I'm afraid you won't have a choice." Giving an almost imperceptible nod to Hawke, his friend drew the six-shooter at his waist while stepping behind the cowboy. With a quick swipe through the air, the butt of his gun landed on the back of the man's head, dropping him to the ground.

A collective groan came from the men on the boardwalk, hoping to see more action. Shane shook his head at their reaction as he knelt by the fallen cowboy.

"Bloodthirsty," he muttered to Hawke, who checked the knot on the man's head.

"The excitement of a crowd."

Hefting the inert body up, the two dragged him into the jail and an empty cell. His eyes opened to slits before closing. A moment later, the cowboy blew out an earsplitting snore, the first of many.

"Should have known he'd be a loud sleeper." Hawke removed his hat, setting it on a hook by the door.

Pouring two cups of hours' old coffee, Shane handed one to Hawke, taking a seat in one of the well-used chairs. Blowing across the hot liquid, he stretched out his legs, crossing them at the ankles. "How's your beautiful wife?"

Hawke hesitated a moment, rubbing his stubbled jaw. "She's pregnant."

Shane darn near dropped the cup, righting it in time not to spill too much. "Pregnant?"

He knew how Hawke felt about having children after losing his first wife and twin sons to ex-Confederate raiders after the war. Knowing how much his wife, Beauty, wanted them, he'd softened a little, but Shane guessed this was a surprise.

"Yep." Hawke focused his attention out the window. Close to midnight, Shane knew there wasn't much for him to see. It was his friend's way of thinking when not ready to talk. Shane stayed silent, waiting him out.

"Don't know how I feel about it." Setting his cup on the desk, Hawke pulled a knife from his pocket, studying the carvings on the ivory handle. "Beauty was scared to tell me." A pained expression crossed his face. "Thought I'd ask her to find a way to get rid of it. I may not be as excited as her, but I'd never do that."

Shane tried to put himself in Hawke's position, but couldn't. He'd never been married. Hadn't lost a wife and children to the treachery of raiders after the war ended. He had lost the woman he planned to marry due to her scheming family. That was nothing compared to what his friend had endured.

"She knows you love her, Hawke. Everyone knows you'd never do anything to hurt her or your children. Be patient with her."

A slight grin appeared on Hawke's face. "Are you giving me marriage advice?"

Chuckling, Shane shook his head. "Never."

The cowboy's snores almost drowned out the sound of the jail door opening. Still wearing his apron and carrying a bar towel in one hand, Paul, the bartender at the Dixie, entered.

"Partners of the cowboy you have locked up are causing trouble. Showed up from Finn's Saloon to find him missing. They're on their way over—" A bullet shattering the window had the tall, muscular man diving for the floor.

Muttering curses while dropping to his belly, Shane and Hawke drew their six-shooters as they inched toward the door. Another shot passed through the broken window to slam into the wall behind Gabe's desk, followed by two more.

"Were they drunk, Paul?" Shane checked the bullets in his gun, knowing each chamber was full.

"More than a little. You know how Finn is. He doesn't care how much they have to drink or how obnoxious they get. All he's after is the money." Three more bullets tore into the wall next to the stove, one piercing the tin coffeepot.

"Wasn't any good anyway," Hawke muttered, moving next to the door. Reaching up, he tugged it open enough to glance outside. "How many were there, Paul?"

Rolling over to sit, he drew his legs up, leaning against a wall. "Three that I saw. All hotheaded and young."

Shane scooted next to Hawke, peering out. "Do you know what brand they ride for?"

"No. For sure it's not Redemption's Edge. Dax and Luke don't tolerate this type of behavior." Paul mentioned the largest ranch in western Montana owned by the Pelletier brothers. "Don't know more than what I've told you."

Opening the door a few more inches, Hawke slammed it shut when several bullets smashed into it. The cowboys' laughter floated through the broken glass, followed by more shots.

Leaning against the wall, Shane stared up at the ceiling, chuckling. "They gotta run out of bullets sometime."

Snorting, Hawke raised to his knees, opening the door once more. "Not if they break into the gunsmith shop."

"They're not that stupid." Shane didn't believe it for a second. Anyone who shot at the jail couldn't be too bright.

"Drop your guns and raise your hands in the air." Deputy Cash Coulter's voice rose above the laughter of the drunken cowboys. "Do it now!" A shot rang out, no doubt from Cash's six-shooter. "Shane and Hawke, you can come out now."

Standing, guns in their hands, the two walked out as Cash herded three men toward the jail.

"Couldn't stand the shooting and yelling any longer," Cash said, herding the cowboys past Shane and Hawke. Motioning to the cells, he locked them inside next to their snoring friend.

One of the cowboys stepped forward, gripping the bars with both hands. "We ain't done nothing except have a good time."

Leaning against a wall, Shane holstered his gun. "And shoot up the jail."

"He's right," another said. "We were just trying to find our friend."

Shane motioned toward the other cell. "You mean, that one?"

The three glanced at the cell next to theirs. They seemed surprised at their friend passed out on a metal bed with a thin mattress.

The one gripping the bars let go, staring at the snoring man. "He never could hold his liquor."

"At least he didn't shoot at someone." Hawke met the gaze of each of the young men. "You boys are in a passel of trouble." Adjusting his hat, he headed for the door. "I'm going to make one more round, then head home to my wife."

Cash started to follow Hawke, then stopped. "You all right here with these reprobates?"

"I'm fine. Dutch will be here anytime, and Zeke not long after. You go back to bed." Shane clasped him on the shoulder. "Thanks for rounding them up."

"Darn cowboys ruined a real nice evening." Cash winked at him before leaving Shane to watch over the cowboys.

Walking to the window, he stepped over the broken glass to peer out the opening. Gabe Evans, Splendor's sheriff, was going to be spitting mad when he came in tomorrow.

Sitting behind the desk, Shane opened a drawer, pulling out a stack of wanted posters. Tracing the thin scar on his left cheek, he studied each face before setting them aside, stilling at one he hadn't seen before.

Rand Sutton. Shane stared into the face of the most vicious outlaw he'd ever met.

While a deputy in Cheyenne, Wyoming, he'd been part of a posse tracking Sutton and his gang. They'd caught up with them not far from the Montana border, killing most, and arresting Sutton and three of his men. Shane had been ordered to guard Sutton during the ride back to Cheyenne. Somehow, they'd missed several members of the gang who'd split off from the main gang. That mistake cost the posse, and the town.

Tried and convicted of murder, Shane thought the violent reign of Rand Sutton had ended. With ropes around their necks, a party of over a dozen gunmen stormed the town, killing several townsfolk, and freeing Sutton and the men who'd gone to jail with him.

Dealing with the carnage left behind, the sheriff had made the decision not to send out another posse. Protests from Shane and a few of the deputies were ignored. The town wanted to mourn their dead and move on.

Putting the other posters away, he continued to study Rand's image. The stories described the man as a giant with a long, black beard, massive arms, and standing almost six-feet-four. In reality, the outlaw had been no more than five-seven, slim of stature, with scrawny arms and legs, and thinning red hair mixed with strands of gray. None of that mattered. Sutton took treachery to a new level, killing women and children when they stood between him and what he wanted.

Reading the brief description, the outlaw was believed to be hiding in The Flat, a lawless town north of Fort Griffin, Texas. Shane had heard it was claimed to be the roughest town in the state, which was saying a lot. Few lawmen ventured into the town, and those who did seldom rode out.

Rubbing his jaw, a chill ran through him. During the trial, Sutton had vowed to kill every man in the posse, pointing his finger at Shane. Two were murdered during the outlaw's escape. Shane had been lucky. Sutton's bullet had missed him by inches before one of the outlaw's men forced him to ride out. Glancing over his shoulder at Shane, the look in the outlaw's eyes had stayed with him from that day until now.

If his calculations were right, Fort Griffin had to be close to two thousand miles from Splendor. Even if Sutton knew where Shane lived, it was a long ride for revenge.

Placing the poster back in the drawer, he leaned back in the chair, debating whether or not to tell Gabe. Several minutes passed before he straightened. Rubbing his eyes, he made his decision.

Shane could see no point in talking with Gabe. Tomorrow, he'd send a message to the colonel at Fort Griffin, requesting any information available on Sutton.

Satisfied with his decision, Shane checked the cells. All were either passed out or asleep. Either way, they weren't going anywhere.

Stalking back to the broken front window, he looked up at a sky blanketed with stars. The view reminded him of days long past when he and the girl he'd planned to marry would stare at the same sky for hours. Fingers entwined, he and Angela would talk about their future, the number of children they'd have, and where they'd live.

Not once had it occurred to Shane the future, which meant so much to him, would never happen.

Chapter Two

Boston, Massachusetts
Two months later

Angela Baldwin sat on a park bench across the street from her former fiancé's lavish home. It had been over five months since she'd returned home. Three since Carson Winslow's body arrived for burial. Edith Winslow, still distraught over her son's death, stayed isolated in her bedroom, leaving it for no more than an hour. Out of necessity, Angela took over directing the household staff, having been trained by Carson's mother.

Sitting at the park, she fingered the sleeves of her black dress, feeling a stab of pain along with a heavy dose of guilt. Angela grieved for Carson. Missed their easy friendship. He'd been a constant in her life since turning eighteen, when her father sent her to Boston to live with the Winslows.

It had been a rough time in her life. Not only had her father forced a separation from her family, but also the man she'd planned to marry.

He'd meant everything to her. One evening, they'd taken one of their many long walks, the next, her father had shuttled her off to Boston. Angela had cried the entire trip, stopping for a short time to meet the Winslows. Once at their magnificent home, and being shown to her bedroom, the tears began again.

Watching the children play in the park, her throat thickened at the memory. Scared, alone, in a strange city, and missing the one person who could've made everything all right. Over time, and without knowing it, Carson's friendship had helped her forget her former life. He'd never been able to erase the memories of the one person she'd always love.

"Angela. I thought that was you." A young woman, close to her age, sat on the bench beside her.

Lifting her face, she tried to match the woman's smile. "Hello, Martha. It's good to see you."

"How are you doing?"

Clasping her hands in her lap, Angela wanted to answer with the truth, knowing she couldn't. "Fine. Better each day."

"And how is Mrs. Winslow? Any improvement?"

Staring down into her lap, she shook her head. "She stays in her room, leaving for a brief time when someone arrives for a social call. I don't know what to do."

"I'm so sorry. What does the doctor say?"

"With her husband and son gone, he's worried she'll give up."

Martha was silent for a long time while Angela's attention moved back to the children. It was hard to remember a time she was so carefree.

"What will you do if she joins her husband?"

It took Angela a moment to realize what Martha meant. "I haven't thought too much about it. Carson had already drawn up a will, naming me the recipient of his estate. His mother didn't protest. She said it would make her life easier not to deal with such things. If something would happen to her, I'd still be required to stay for a time. Then?" She shrugged, not wanting to dwell on something she didn't want to happen.

"It's sad to think of such a vibrant, intelligent woman giving up on life. Perhaps if you and Carson had married, she might not be so distressed. What I mean is, you'd have been her daughter-in-law. Now, you're just..." Martha's voice trailed off.

"The woman Carson would've married if he hadn't been murdered."

"If Mrs. Winslow does pass, traveling might ease the pain from all you've been through, Angela. The problem is, you're a single woman and shouldn't consider traveling alone. If you and Carson had married, then you'd be a widow, and—" Martha slapped a hand over her mouth.

"It would've been acceptable," Angela finished for her.

Nodding, Martha dropped her hand. "I'm sorry. I don't know what's gotten into me. It's such a morbid topic, and I'm not making it better for you."

Angela offered a wan smile, which didn't light her face. "Please don't worry yourself. I know my place, what is expected of me. When Edith improves, I'll speak with her about traveling. She may be willing to go with me, or suggest a companion."

"I could be your companion."

Angela's head whipped toward Martha, jaw dropping. "What?"

"Well, if you decide to travel and don't have a companion, I could go."

Shifting on the bench, Angela's eyes sparked with interest. "What about your parents?"

"If they knew I was accompanying you, I'm certain they'd be open to it."

"You'd put off marriage to go with me?"

Martha snorted an unladylike laugh. "Marriage doesn't appear to be in my future. I'm twenty-two, plain, never been courted, and have no prospects. I'm facing a grim future, Angela."

"Twenty-two isn't old. Why, many women are waiting until their mid-twenties or later to marry." Angela thought of Martha's father, a disagreeable man in every way. She couldn't imagine anyone would want to be a part of their family, forced to deal with her unpleasant father.

"Because they are in the same position as I am. Believe me, I know about waiting to marry. Most times, men choose those women because they're widowed and have children. They aren't looking for a true companion as much as a nanny." Biting her lower lip, a wistful expression crossed her face. "Perhaps traveling will improve my chances of meeting a suitable man."

Angela thought of the only man she'd ever loved. It had been almost seven months since they'd seen each other for the first time in six years. The reunion hadn't been planned, nor expected.

She and Carson had been traveling west to San Francisco when they came across Splendor, Montana. He'd been intrigued with the town and the people. Many had moved from the east, some with wealth, most without. The town benefited from local mines and prosperous cattle ranches.

There was one bank, which interested Carson a great deal. He believed the town could benefit from a second, funded by wealthy families from Boston and New York. Her fiancé had even sent several telegrams home to gauge the interest. Before being murdered, he'd received a few replies, all stating they were intrigued, and requested a meeting with Carson when they returned.

Shaking her head, she forced herself to focus on Martha. "I met some good men while traveling west. We didn't stay long in cities on the trip out, so I'm unable to give you an impression of the men. However, we did spend considerable time in the western Montana town of Splendor."

Martha's eyes lit with interest. "Did you enjoy your stay?"

"Yes, very much. Then Carson was kidnapped and murdered. My entire life changed." She fell silent, not wanting to dwell on the ruin of a future. It was the second time her life had been snatched away. First, by a greedy father, then by a murderer who hadn't been found.

"Would you ever consider returning?" Martha's voice held a hint of excitement.

Angela again fingered the edges of her sleeve. When the stage left Splendor to return her to Boston, she recalled watching out the window, hoping to see the man who'd always held her heart. He hadn't appeared, her heart cracking on the knowledge she'd never see him again. Or would she?

"Someday. Right now, my duty is to Edith. Until she's well, I can't consider leaving."

"Then we shall have to pray she recovers soon."

Returning home, Angela stood outside the grand home Mr. Winslow had built for his wife when Carson was born. Three stories, taking up half a city block, most women would be thrilled to live in such a palace. Although grateful for all the family had done for her, the house had always felt sterile and cold.

Not because of the furniture and magnificent art. As much as Carson loved his parents, they'd always been stiff and formal around their son. The same reserved attitudes had carried over to her. The only warmth had come from Carson.

Her throat tightened at the loss of her best friend. They'd both known their marriage would've been one of deep caring and commitment, not the love each had craved. A few years older than Angela, he'd been well aware the time had come to marry and produce heirs.

It had taken months after his father's death for Carson to convince her how well they suited. His points had been reasonable, the benefits to her beyond her imagination. But she'd held out. Love could do that to a person. Make them wish for things no longer possible.

When she'd stopped resisting, Carson had been ecstatic, announcing their betrothal within days. All she'd asked was to put off the ceremony for a year. He'd agreed, deciding to confront the delay with a trip to the Pacific Ocean.

"Are you coming in, miss?"

Looking up to find Joseph, the Winslows' butler, standing on the front stoop, she walked up the steps. "Yes. It's such a beautiful day, I wanted to spend a few more minutes outside." Turning once more toward the park, she was surprised to see Martha still sitting on the bench.

Stepping inside, she removed her bonnet and gloves, handing them to the butler. "How is Edith doing?"

"Not good, I'm afraid. She refused breakfast. Not even taking a cup of tea." The short, rotund man, who'd been with the family since Carson's birth, glanced toward the staircase. "May I be frank?"

"Of course, Joseph."

Clearing his throat, he paused a moment, glancing around to see if any of the other servants were within hearing distance. "The madam no longer cares about anything, miss. The deaths of her husband and son have taken away her will to live. I find myself afraid for her."

"As do I. Was the doctor here while I was gone?"

"He sent a messenger to say he'd be visiting patients outside of the city today, but will be by tomorrow. May I get you tea, miss?"

"After all this time, can't you find it within yourself to call me Angela?"

Flushing, Joseph let out a sigh. "We've discussed this before, miss. Mrs. Winslow insists the staff not use your given names. I'll prepare your tea. Will you be in the parlor?"

"The library. First, I'm going to check on Edith."

"I was upstairs not long before you returned, miss. The madam was sleeping. You may want to wait until after you've finished your tea."

"You're right. I can help her dress, and maybe convince her to join us downstairs for luncheon."

"Perhaps." His voice conveyed the doubt he felt about the older woman leaving her bedroom.

"Well, all I can do is try. I'll take the tea now, Joseph."

Scanning the library shelves as she'd done a hundred times in the past, Angela selected a book she'd read many times. *Pride and Prejudice* always took her mind off her worries. She hoped it would do the same today.

Taking the overstuffed chair by a window looking out to the flower garden in the back, she opened the book. Immersing herself in the story, she didn't notice when Joseph set her tea on a nearby table.

Not long afterward, the story became a blur as her mind traveled west to Splendor. An image of the man she'd known since childhood took hold. The book forgotten, she allowed herself time to remember. Not just their few encounters in the western town, but the love they'd shared while growing up. He'd become her world. At eighteen, he'd proposed. It had been the best day of her life.

"Miss Angela!" Joseph's frantic voice pierced through her thoughts, causing her to look up. Seeing his panic, she jumped up, ignoring the book landing at her feet.

"What is it?"

Wringing his hands in a motion she'd never seen him do, he pointed upstairs. "It's Mrs. Winslow..." His voice faltered.

Stepping in front of him, she touched his arm. "What about her?"

"The madam...she won't wake up."

Chapter Three

Splendor

"We need more deputies." Gabe Evans sipped from his cup, enjoying the first of the coffee shipped to him from New York to the jail. He'd ordered it months earlier, losing the first batch when the stagecoach from Cheyenne had been attacked. Somewhere out there, a group of outlaws were experiencing the best coffee available in the country.

Shane grinned, setting down his empty cup. "Can't remember ever having such good coffee, Gabe."

Caleb Covington and Mack Mackey nodded in agreement from their spots across the room. What they'd had before couldn't even be called coffee.

"How many deputies are you thinking?"

Gabe looked at Shane, his mouth twisting as he considered his answer. "Two, maybe three. Experienced, the same as you three before you arrived in Splendor. I've already spoken with Hawke, Hex, and Zeke. I'll be speaking with the rest of the deputies."

Caleb rubbed his jaw. "I might know of a Texas Ranger in Austin. The last I heard, he was looking for a change."

"There's a deputy in Cheyenne who might be interested," Shane said. "I tried to get him to ride north when I left, but he wasn't ready."

Mack shook his head. "I'll think on it. We should ask Dom Lucero, maybe the Pelletiers. Both were rangers before inheriting their ranch."

Drumming his fingers on the desk, Gabe nodded. "I'll speak with Dom. Dax and Luke left Austin a long time ago. Let's do what we can first, then I'll speak with them." Reaching into his desk, he pulled out the stack of wanted posters. Flipping through them, he left one on the desk.

Shane glanced at the image, a lump forming in his throat.

"Sheriff Parker Sterling, in Big Pine, received a telegraph from a lawman in Texas." Sliding the poster toward them, his finger stabbed at the name. "Rand Sutton. Have any of you heard of him?"

"I have." Shane shot a quick look at the others. "We arrested him when I was a deputy in Wyoming. He was convicted of murder and scheduled to hang. Before we could get him up the steps of the gallows, he escaped when a group of his men rode into town." He let out a breath, remembering the carnage. "Several of the townsfolk died. The sheriff decided not to go after them. Rand Sutton's the most vicious man I've ever met. What did Sterling say about him?"

Gabe studied Shane for several seconds, resting his arms on the desk to lean forward. "The Texas lawman said Rand left a place called The Flat near Fort Griffin."

"A town populated with outlaws," Shane interjected.

Gabe nodded. "Seems he mentioned going to Cheyenne, then Montana to a few people. It got back to the lawman. He and Sterling go way back, so he sent the telegram. Is there anything else you can tell us about Sutton?"

Scrubbing a hand down his face, Shane breathed out a weary breath. "When we captured Rand and a few of his men, I was given responsibility of making certain Sutton got to the jail to stand trial. He kept staring at me. After the conviction, he vowed to kill every man in the posse. We believed it was an empty threat, knowing he'd hang the following day."

He stood, a sense of urgency gripping him. "We have to send a telegram to the sheriff in Cheyenne. Some of those in the posse are still there."

"Go ahead, but stay vigilant. Somehow, Sutton found out you are here in Montana. Maybe not where, but in the territory."

Lips thinning, he offered a slow nod. "Sorry, Gabe. I never thought what happened with Rand would come back to haunt me."

"It's not your fault, Shane. As you said, the man is a vicious killer. He holds a grudge. I believe he heard about you from someone who traveled through Splendor. Someone who landed in The Flat."

"Makes sense." Caleb picked up the poster again. "We need to notify more than just the deputies."

"I'll be talking to Noah." Gabe mentioned his best friend since childhood. "Also Nick and several others, but not the entire town. They've been through a lot over the last few months. No sense causing a panic."

"The people in Splendor are tough," Mack said. "I'd suggest waiting until Shane gets a response from the sheriff in Cheyenne. If Sutton does show up there, we'll know it's time to include the town."

"I'll go send off the telegram." Shane stepped outside, coming to a halt as he looked up and down the street.

Late afternoon and the town had quieted after a busy day. A few wagons, and single riders, moved along the street, music from the tinny piano in Finn's flowed out the batwing doors. He'd grown to love Splendor. Hoped one day to fall in love, marry, and have a family.

Mind going to the woman who still held his heart, he brutally shoved it aside. Her life was in Boston. He thought of the day she'd left on the stage to return home. For a brief moment, he'd considered going after her, asking her to stay. Months later, he wondered if the decision to let her go was the right one.

Shaking off the regret, he sent the telegram. Impressing on the clerk, Bernie Griggs, the urgency of getting any response to Gabe or one of the deputies.

Leaving the office, Shane did something rare for him. Entering the Dixie, he went straight to the bar.

"You observing, or want a drink?" Paul cleaned the bar in front of Shane, waiting.

"A whiskey, and leave the bottle."

Lifting a brow, the bartender stilled. "You sure? I don't believe I've ever seen you drink more than a couple whiskeys."

"I'm sure."

Resting his arms on the bar, Shane stared down at the dark liquid in the glass. If Rand Sutton came to Splendor for revenge, it would be because of him, and any deaths would fall at his feet. Leaving the town he loved wasn't his choice, but riding out would eliminate the danger.

A hand landed on his shoulder, squeezing. Glancing into the mirror behind the bar, his gaze locked on the image of Hawke beside him.

"A full bottle? I understand what's going through your mind. I also know whiskey isn't the answer." Motioning to Paul for a glass, he filled it from Shane's bottle. Saying nothing more, he stood next to his friend and fellow deputy.

Minutes passed before Shane spoke. "I may have to leave Splendor."

"You going after your woman?"

Brows drawing together, he shifted to face Hawke. "Don't know what you're talking about."

"Anyone with eyes could see how you looked at her. What I don't understand is why you didn't stop her from leaving."

Picking up the glass, Shane downed the contents in one gulp. Feeling the burn in his chest and stomach, he reached out to grab the bottle, stopping when Hawke gripped his wrist.

"Whiskey isn't the answer."

Yanking his arm away, Shane tamped down the anger aimed at Hawke. His friend wasn't the problem. Nor was the woman.

"I won't be leaving because of any woman. Rand Sutton."

"What about him?"

"If I ride out, the chances are he won't come to Splendor."

Hawke considered his reason for a moment before throwing back his head in laughter. "That's the darndest thing I've ever heard come out of your mouth."

The anger returned, his face turning a deep red. Tightening his grip on the edge of the bar, he stomped down his urge to punch Hawke. "Why's that?"

"Because that varmint is going to come here whether you leave or not. Sutton isn't going to know if you ride out, Shane. He's got no one here to get a telegram to him. Hell, we don't know for sure if he's riding this way. The outlaw may be riding toward the Dakotas, or Oklahoma, or any of a dozen other places."

Staring at his empty glass, Shane's anger faded. "What if he does come to Splendor?"

"Then we'll need you here." Shoving his glass away, Hawke pushed away from the bar. "As I said, we don't even know if Sutton is coming this direction."

The doors of the saloon slammed open, drawing everyone's attention. Rushing inside, Bernie waved the telegram in his hand, bouncing on his toes. "Deputy. You got a reply from Cheyenne."

Gabe read the telegram Shane tossed on the desk, frowning. "Doesn't tell us much. The sheriff in Cheyenne has been alerted that Sutton may be riding to Wyoming. He's taken precautions, and will send another telegram if the outlaw rides into Cheyenne." Gabe held up the telegram. "Do you mind if I keep this?"

"It's best if you do." Lowering himself into a chair, Shane rubbed his forehead. "Maybe I should leave Splendor. The town will be safe if I'm not here."

Eyes narrowing on his deputy, Gabe shook his head. "If he's out for revenge, Sutton will come here regardless. He won't know you've left. If he arrives and finds you gone, he'll still be a threat. I'll need all my men, including you."

Shane snorted out a chuckle.

Lifting a brow, Gabe motioned for him to explain.

"Hawke said the same."

Slapping his hands on the desk, Gabe stood. "I'll bet the other deputies would, too. I'm heading home to dinner and my family. You're welcome to join us."

"Thanks, Gabe, but I'm heading home." It was his one day off, and he'd already spent enough time at the jail. Tomorrow, he'd go back to his usual night shift.

An unexpected sorrow settled over him on the walk home. He and Hawke had shared the two bedroom house until his fellow deputy had married, moving in with Beauty. It was too big for one man. Living alone had never bothered him in the past, didn't believe he and Hawke could make it work. They had, and it had been harder than

Shane expected seeing him move out with his few belongings.
Shane should speak with Noah Brandt about moving into one of the smaller homes the man had built in town. He and his wife, Abby, had been generous when planning the houses. Large bedrooms, living room, and kitchen, unlike anything Shane had rented in his travels.

Walking past Caleb and May's place, he spotted his home on the next street. Unlike his fellow deputies, there were no lights on, nothing on the stove, and a fireplace devoid of heat.

Opening the door, he walked inside, pausing to look around. The furniture had come from Noah's warehouse. Same with most of the pots and pans in the kitchen. It occurred to him the house was a perfect place to bring a wife.

Instead of starting dinner, he dropped into a chair, rubbing his eyes. Marriage hadn't been a subject he considered for over six years. He had his chance once, and lost it.

Yet he still longed for a woman to share his future, and children to pass along the legacy of his heritage. He suspected his mixed cultures of Irish, Cherokee, and Spanish had played a part in losing his first love.

Closing his eyes, Shane thought of the single women in Splendor. Carrie Galloway and Georgina Wise both worked at the clinic. He couldn't imagine himself with the outspoken Georgie, but Carrie was worth considering.

Rose Keenan had accepted the job as the town's teacher, starting in the fall. Sweet and kind, she'd make a wonderful mother. Amelia Newhall, also a school teacher, worked at the boardinghouse restaurant. She was also a woman he could grow to love.

Three possible women to share his life. All educated, pretty, who'd come to Splendor looking for a new start. Perhaps it was time to put the past behind him, and look toward a new future.

Chapter Four

Boston

Rain pummeled the black umbrellas, the day as gloomy as the reason dozens of people braved the storm to show their respects. Many believed Edith Winslow had been the backbone of the family. A gentle woman with a core of steel and generous nature, she would be missed.

Lifting her head to see the workers lower the casket, Angela realized the service had ended. Most of those honoring Edith were rushing to their buggies, jumping over pools of water in their hurry to find cover.

Martha stood beside her, the young woman's presence providing support Angela appreciated. Joseph, and two other members of their staff, had stayed. The cook and another woman were at the house, preparing refreshments for the expected visitors.

Angela knew her place was at the home, welcoming those who'd endured the inclement weather to honor Edith. The sound of the casket hitting the soggy ground signaled the end of her vigil. Still, her feet didn't move.

"Miss. We should return to the house."

Giving a slow nod at Joseph's encouraging voice, she turned away from the grave. "We should go."

Holding the umbrella, he kept pace next to Angela on the way to the buggy. Martha followed, heart heavy at her friend's loss.

Angela's unseeing eyes stared at the passing houses, her mind beginning to move from mourning to the decisions facing her. The Winslows' attorney had visited the day after Edith's death, expressing his condolences, and requesting a meeting the day after the services. She didn't look forward to their discussion tomorrow.

Hearing the front door close, a tear rolled down Angela's cheek. Unmoving from her seat in the Winslows' parlor, she considered her future.

Edith had been generous with her estate. A large investment account, including cash, had been left to Angela. Along with the funds left to her by Carson, she'd never have to worry about her future.

A smaller amount went to Joseph and the household staff. The mansion in Boston would be closed, the family's banker already supplying the name of a qualified buyer. The proceeds would be split fifty percent to Angela, twenty to various charities, with the remainder split between Edith's loyal employees. She would be allowed to stay in the house for ninety days.

Edith's provisions were more than generous, far beyond any expectations Angela held.

"Are you all right, miss?"

Throat thick, she nodded.

"Perhaps you would enjoy tea?"

Again, she nodded, unable to speak for the emotion spearing through her. Angela had never expected such generosity.

She thought of her family, the father who'd sent her north. Edith had always promised to explain the reasons the Winslows had taken her into their home. Though the older woman had given hints, she'd gone silent after Carson's death.

A minor provision in the will left Angela all of Edith's personal effects. She hoped answers would be found when she sorted the woman's letters.

"Here you are, miss." Joseph set down a cup of tea. "Would there be anything else?"

Forcing a small, mischievous grin, she met his expectant gaze. "Please call me Angela."

Opening his mouth, he closed it for a moment before replying. "Would Miss Angela be all right?"

This time, the smile wasn't forced. "Yes, it would."

"Very well...Miss Angela."

Alone with her tea, she allowed some time to consider the future, and what she'd do with hers. Spotting Edith's writing desk across the room, she rose, walking to where the older woman composed letters and responded to invitations. Angela doubted Edith would've kept anything of value inside. She had to go through it at some point in the next three months, might as well do it now.

Returning for her tea, she took a sip before sitting down and opening the center drawer of the desk. Typical of Edith, the contents were well-organized. Personalized paper on the right, envelopes on the left, an extra fountain pen in the middle. Removing the drawer, she looked into the open space, finding nothing. The other two drawers held nothing personal. Picking up her tea, she thought of other places Edith would've kept her private correspondence. The answer struck as a bolt of lightning.

Hurrying upstairs, Angela stopped at the open door to Edith's bedroom. On one wall stood an exquisite Danish mahogany bookcase her husband had given her at their tenth anniversary. The bottom half was a cabinet, which locked.

She'd once witnessed Edith sliding a box onto a shelf before locking the door and pocketing the key. Drawing in a breath, she exhaled, her gaze wandering over the room.

Two bed stands, a dresser, vanity, lounge chair, two wardrobes placed side-to-side, and the bookcase. Her instincts told her what she sought would be in the bottom cabinet of the bookcase. The locked cabinet.

Checking the bed stands, then moving to the vanity, she turned to study the dresser. Stepping across the room, she started at the top. Rifling through the contents, Angela was careful to leave the contents as she found them.

Reaching the bottom drawer, she searched it the same as the others. This time, her hand touched a velvet box at the back. Opening it, she let out a slow breath.

Picking it up, she knelt in front of the cabinet. The double doors opened to reveal a fabric covered, rectangular box. Hands shaking, she set it on her lap, removing the lid.

The contents surprised her. Instead of letters, she spotted several pieces of broken jewelry, a photograph of the family before Angela arrived, a teacup, and several tiny figurines. She almost missed the paper lining at the bottom.

Lifting it, being careful not to damage the contents, she stared at an envelope showing a stamp dated a few months before her father sent her to Boston. Standing, she carried the box and letter to the bed and sat down.

Her fingers trembled as she removed the letter inside. Opening it, her breath caught, recognizing the bold, slanted writing. Her father's script.

Heart thudding in her chest, she read. By the time she finished, tears streamed down her face. More than six years after being sent away, Angela found her answers.

༺∽༻

"I'm so excited. Forgive me if I say or do anything that embarrasses you." Martha stood on the train platform with Angela, a satchel at their feet.

Two weeks after finding the letter, Angela had finalized her affairs, packed, and bought two tickets to Cheyenne, Wyoming.

"You could never do anything to embarrass me, Martha. If it helps, I was just as excited before traveling west with Carson."

Angela remembered being unable to sleep the night before they left, her feet tapping on the platform while waiting to board. The trip would always be emblazoned on her mind.

Chicago, St. Louis, Denver, and Cheyenne, all presented a different view of life outside Boston. She hadn't picked a favorite, each one special in its own way. She hoped Martha felt the same during their trip.

The train's whistle signaled they could board. Grabbing the satchel, Martha flashed a brilliant smile at Angela. "Here we go."

Several days passed, the train stopping to let off and take on passengers. The newness hadn't worn off for Martha, her enthusiasm as strong as when she'd boarded.

Angela kept busy reading, glancing outside every few minutes, observing the different people on the train. She made a mental list of those traveling.

A pastor and his wife, who'd boarded in Boston, hadn't disembarked. A young married couple with two children joined them in Chicago, leaving in St. Louis, the boy and girl chattering the entire time.

Two men wearing six-shooters took seats across from them in Denver. They spoke in low whispers, making her believe they were planning something nefarious. Three rows forward sat a tall, rotund man in an expensive suit. His back was ramrod straight, gaze fixed straight ahead as the train rolled along. He disembarked in Cheyenne, the same as Angela and Martha, never uttering a word to anyone.

The stage to Splendor didn't leave until the following day, allowing them to spend the night in a hotel. Taking baths, they dressed for supper.

"Do they have the same food as at home?" Martha stopped in front of each store, peering inside before moving on.

"Steak, roast, chicken, potatoes, and depending on the time of year, vegetables and fruit. Some fresh and some canned. The railroad brings in provisions from the east and west. The food is always quite good."

Entering the restaurant recommended by the hotel, they were shown to a table against a wall. Several minutes after ordering, two men walked inside, looking as if they'd been riding for days or weeks. They sat down at a table a few feet from the women.

"Aren't those the men who were on the train?" Martha nodded toward them without looking.

Angela wasn't as reticent, her gaze narrowing on them. "Yes."

"Do you think they're real cowboys?"

When the two slipped out of their coats, placing them on hooks near their table, Angela sucked in a breath. Both wore badges.

"I believe they're Texas Rangers."

"Really?" The question squeaked out louder than Martha intended, drawing glances from the men. Face

already flushed, it darkened further when the lawmen dipped their chins at her.
"Don't look now, but they have badges pinned to their shirts. I'm certain they're the ones worn by the rangers." While in Splendor, Angela had been told several former rangers lived in and around the town. She'd heard many stories about the respected group of lawmen. Most good, some not so much. There'd even been a dime novel written about them.
Leaning forward, lowering her voice, Martha's eyes sparked in anticipation. "Perhaps we'll get to meet them."
Angela looked down to clear her amused expression. "It's doubtful. There's no one to make introductions."
Shoulders slumping, Martha's face fell. "You're right. I don't know what I was thinking."
The women quieted when the server placed heaping plates of food before them. "More coffee?" When both shook their heads, the woman grinned. "Let me know if you change your mind."
"Thank you." Martha stared down at a plate heaped with large slices of meatloaf, a huge portion of potatoes, and a mixture of beans and carrots. "There's so much."
"Mine is large enough for two men. Maybe three." Fork in hand, Angela scooped up a portion of the potatoes, sliding them into her mouth. "Hmm..." A grin tipped up the corners of her mouth. "These are delicious."
"So is the meatloaf. We may have to stay longer to finish everything."

Angela thought the same. Lifting a bite of meatloaf to her mouth, the fork dropped to the floor as the front window splintered before a bullet tore into her arm.

Chapter Five

Splendor

Shane ran his hand over the wood counter toward the sink, stepping back. "It's real fine work, Noah. You built this by yourself?"

"Gabe came out a few times, as did some other men, but the rest I did. Took a while." Noah took in the dirt on the wood planks and spiderwebs in the ceiling. "Haven't been out here for a couple months to clean. Abby and I used to come out every week, bringing Gabriel with us after he was born. With our businesses, and Abby's pregnancy, we don't get out here as often."

Shane waved off the comments. "Cleaning won't be a problem, Noah. The workmanship is impressive. Can I see the rest?"

Noah left the kitchen. "You've already seen the living room. There's just one bedroom and a water closet. It's primitive compared to those at the St. James Hotel, but Abby wanted something in the cabin when we were first married. So..." He shrugged, opening the door to the bedroom, allowing Shane to move past him. "I built it so another could be added over there." Noah pointed to one wall.

Walking around the oversized room, Shane already knew he wanted the cabin.

"The water closet is through this door. It's small, but does the job."

Shane glanced over Noah's shoulder. "Better than what I'd expect in a cabin out this far."

Noah chuckled, closing the door. "I built it when her father, King Tolbert, made it clear he'd never approve of me for her husband. When he died, Abby inherited his estate. At the time, it was obvious I'd never be able to give her the life she deserved." Shaking his head, he walked to the front door. "The darn woman wouldn't leave it alone. No matter what I said, she kept coming around. You already know Abby won the battle."

Shane clasped Noah's shoulder. "I doubt you put up too much of a fight."

Smiling without responding, Noah headed to the barn. "Doesn't look like it from the outside, but there are four stalls and a tack room."

Taking a quick look around, Shane turned back to Noah. "What do you want for it?"

Rubbing his sandy blond stubble, Noah's mouth twisted. When he answered, Shane's eyes lit with relief. Holding out his hand, the men shook, the deal done.

On the ride back, they spoke of Noah's growing family and the need to build more houses for the growing population before the conversation turned to Rand Sutton.

"Gabe says the man may be headed here. He told me you've met him."

Shane's hand on the reins tightened. "I was part of the posse which arrested him in Wyoming. After his trial, he escaped, but not before threatening the men in the posse and killing two of them. Both were in the group who arrested him."

"Makes sense he'd be after you. If Sutton does make the mistake of coming to Splendor, you'll have a good number of men with you."

Shane gave a brisk nod, not wanting Noah to see the emotion in his eyes. He'd never imagined this amount of support from any town.

They continued in silence, reaching the edge of town minutes later. Reining up outside the livery, they dismounted, Noah opening the gate. Before they could enter, a shout came from behind them.

"Deputy Banderas!"

Both men turned to see Bernie Griggs running toward them, a telegram waving in the air. "You have another message."

Taking the paper from Bernie's hand, Shane frowned as he read it. Jaw clenched, he handed it to Noah.

After a quick read, he gave it back to Shane. "Guess we have our answer about the direction Sutton is riding."

Shane felt the burn in his stomach as tension enveloped him. "North, right toward Splendor."

Ruby Walsh, the owner of the Grand Palace, leaned against the bar, her focus on the men, and one woman, sitting together. Gabe had come to her an hour earlier, asking her to close the Palace so he and his deputies could talk without interruption.

She'd hesitated at first, requiring an explanation before shooing out paying customers. Hearing the reason, Ruby agreed, preparing a spot for the thirteen people. Drinks would be on Gabe.

Cole Santori, the newest deputy, took a seat between Shane and Hawke. He hadn't been in Splendor long. Still, the threat Gabe outlined made his blood run cold.

"Two days ago, Sutton and his men rode into Cheyenne, shot up the town, wounding three townsfolk and killing a deputy. One, a young woman who'd arrived on the day's train."

"The deputy had been part of the posse," Shane added to Gabe's explanation.

Hawke rested an arm over the back of his chair. "Did they hit the bank?"

Gabe shook his head, handing Hawke the telegram. "The sheriff didn't mention it. The odds are Sutton is on his way to Splendor. That's why we're here. We have to prepare ourselves, and the town, in case he does ride in."

Shane rolled out a large map of the area. Noah had prepared it not long after arriving in town, adding businesses and ranches as more people moved into the area.

Gabe stood, leaning over the map. "Besides the people here, several others are willing to be lookouts. Some, such as Noah and Nick, will position themselves once our spotters see Sutton and his men. I'm going to speak with Dax and Luke to see if they have men to spare."

"They'll never get here in time, Gabe."

"You may be right, Shane. If Sutton stops in Big Pine, the sheriff will send a telegram to me when the outlaws ride out. We'll send a rider to the Pelletier ranch. There's a good chance their men will arrive before Sutton."

Using his finger, Gabe pointed to several locations around Splendor. "These are the best places for shooters. Here and here are where I plan to post lookouts."

"Who are you posting in those locations, Gabe?" Beth Evans, a deputy and Gabe's sister-in-law, asked.

"We'll need several people, as most have businesses to run. Amos Henderson volunteered for as much time as we need. Ruth Paige offered. Reverend Paige requested she be used for no more than two hours a day. Silas Jenks can help after he closes the lumber mill each day. Toby Archer, who helps Noah in the tack shop, can do the same as Silas."

As Gabe spoke, Ruby made her way to the table, listening as he named a few more people. "I'd like to help." All heads turned to look at her. "Well, I do have eyes, and my own binoculars." She smiled at them. "And I can shoot."

Gabe's features softened. "Ruby, we would appreciate your help. Don't think you'll need a gun, though."

"Anytime between ten in the morning and three o'clock, Sheriff." Satisfied, she whirled around, returning to her place at the bar.

Narrowing his gaze on Beau Davis, Gabe cleared his throat. "You should know Caro has volunteered."

His wife's name had Beau's eyes widening. "Well, you can just forget about using her."

"She's bored, Beau."

He shot a look at his best friend, Cash Coulter. "She tell you that?"

"Told Allie," Cash mentioned his wife. "She would hire her at the dress shop, but Nora Jackson is there most days. All we need are lookouts, Beau. Maybe talk to Caro about it."

Pinching the bridge of his nose, Beau nodded, the others trying to control their grins.

Caleb leaned back in his chair. "That's five, six if Caro's included, Gabe. We're going to need more."

Mack stood, picked up his chair, swinging it around. Sitting, he rested his arms on the back. "No reason we can't help when we're not on the streets."

"He's right, Gabe." Hex stared down at the map. "Most of us have the time."

"I agree," Beth added. "When Chan's in town, I'm certain he'll do whatever is needed."

"Between his U.S. Marshal job and working with Dom Lucero, you two already have too little time together." Beth opened her mouth to reply, stopping when Gabe held up his hand. "But I'll speak with him."

If Gabe were truthful, he'd insist Beth move in with him and Lena. Their house had plenty of room. Even though she was a deputy, he didn't like his sister-in-law putting herself in danger. Knowing she'd put up a fight if he mentioned it, Gabe turned his attention back to what still needed to be decided.

"All right. Let's talk about spreading the word to those who don't know about Sutton."

Near Fort Laramie, Wyoming

Rand Sutton took another swig of whiskey from the bottle he'd stuffed into his saddlebags, irritation swelling at the antics of his men. He regretted bringing so many young guns into his gang. Reckless and wild, with more enthusiasm than experience. The combination would get some of them killed.

Not that their deaths mattered. They meant no more to him than the whores he visited when the urge struck.

"Hey, Rand. You gonna drink from the bottle or just fondle it?" The young outlaw howled at his own joke.

Not answering, Rand set the bottle down, stretching out his legs. Maybe he was wrong. Those boys dancing around the fire might be the death of him.

He'd learned long ago to block out the foolish antics of the miscreants in his gang. Anger didn't solve anything. At least, that's what his mother always told him. His experience told Rand otherwise. Most decisions he made were born out of rage.

Such as his journey across country to kill the men who'd hunted his gang down, arresting him and a few of his men. The convictions for murder and bank robbery were inconvenient. He'd had complete faith the remaining members of his gang would liberate him.

What fueled his pursuit of those in the posse was the death of his best friend. He'd seen the deputy who'd fired the killing shot at Hoot. The same deputy had ridden beside Rand on the way to Cheyenne, escorted him from the jail to the courthouse, ushering him back to the cell after his conviction.

Shane Banderas. Rand would never forget the man's name. He'd spent many nights thinking about how to kill the man. Slow and painful was the final choice.

It had taken months of asking questions before learning the deputy had left Cheyenne. An outlaw who'd passed through Splendor before traveling south to The Flat provided Banderas's location...for a hefty payment.

Finishing his business in Texas, Rand had rounded up the remnants of his gang, added a few more men, and ridden north. A slow smile formed, knowing in less than a week, he'd face the man who'd killed Hoot.

His punishment would not be swift.

Chapter Six

The stage hit another of a thousand ruts on the trail to Splendor. Angela's left arm struck the trim around a window, an unintentional groan escaping before she could stop it. Sitting next to her, Martha's face clouded in compassion.

"Are you all right?"

Angela nodded, checking the still healing gunshot wound, confirming it wasn't bleeding.

"Do you want some of the laudanum the doctor gave you?"

"No. The pain is better than the way I feel taking the medicine."

"You're looking much better today." Martha's poor attempt at bolstering Angela's spirits didn't succeed.

Angela snorted out a chuckle. "You are such a good friend. We both know I look as if I've risen from the dead. I'm hoping my appearance will improve before reaching Splendor."

Shifting on the bench seat, Martha tilted her head to the side. "You've never told me why we're going to Splendor. Is it because that's where Carson died?" She grimaced, letting out a groan. "There I go again."

Angela knew what she meant. Martha had a habit of speaking before thinking. "The reason does have something to do with what happened. Also because it's a charming town with some exceptional people."

"A charming town in the frontier? It's a little hard to believe after traveling through towns made up of tents and rundown shacks."

Angela thought of Splendor and its people. She'd been surprised when arriving with Carson. The town didn't look at all like the other frontier towns they'd visited. The one exception was Big Pine, but even it didn't have the same charm as Splendor.

"You'll have to see the town for yourself. There's a church and community building at one end, the schoolhouse at the other. There's a wonderful dress shop, and an emporium with items you'd expect in Boston. We'll be staying at the St. James Hotel. One of the owners is a member of the Evans family in New York."

Martha's eyes widened. "Do you mean the hoteliers?"

"Yes. I heard Gabe Evans, who's also the sheriff, inherited the hotels when his uncle died. He travels east at least once a year to visit his properties." She thought of Gabe's wife, Lena. The woman had reached out to her after Carson disappeared. They'd met for lunch more than once before Angela left Splendor. "The St. James is named after Gabe's uncle."

"He's who you meant when you said the town had exceptional people."

"Gabe is one of them, but there are others." Angela thought of the Pelletiers, Nick and Suzanne Barnett, Noah Brandt, and the women who owned the emporium. "I'd like to stay for a while before traveling to San Francisco."

Martha smiled, her eyes alight with anticipation. "Your plans are mine, Angela. This is all a great adventure, and I want to experience everything."

The stage hit a deep hole in the trail. Angela yelped when her arm struck the window for a second time. The two elderly passengers across from her and Martha almost tumbled to the floor, righting themselves to slide back onto the seat. Straightening her dress, the older woman looked at her husband.

"How long until we reach Big Pine?"

Lacing his fingers through hers, he sighed. She'd asked the same question several times since leaving Cheyenne. "I believe the driver told us we'd be there tomorrow morning, dear."

"Will we stop before then?" He glanced at Angela and Martha, giving a slight shrug.

"We should have at least two stops before then," Angela answered. "The driver won't allow us much time at either. As I recall, we'll eat supper at one of them, so that will be a longer stop."

"You've been this way before, miss?"

"Yes, sir. Not quite a year ago, my fiancé and I traveled west from Boston. We took the same route as Martha and I are doing now."

"Did you see Indians?" The woman's voice rose in alarm.

"No, ma'am. We were told there might be some between Cheyenne and Big Pine, then again from Big Pine to Splendor, but we didn't see any." A small smile lifted the corners of Angela's mouth. "My fiancé was quite disappointed."

"He's not traveling with you now?"

"No, ma'am. He, um...never made it home."

Martha slipped her arm through Angela's. Except for the sounds of the stage, the coach grew quiet. Darting her gaze outside, she gasped.

"Are those...are they..." Wide eyes moved to each of the passengers. "Could they be...Indians?"

All four moved to look out the window. "I do believe they are." Angela glanced at Martha, whose lips were pressed together. "They seem to be watching us. There must be a dozen of them."

Martha swallowed the fear knotting in her throat. "As long as they don't get any closer."

They continued to watch as the stage moved along, putting more distance between them and the Indians. Several miles passed before they were satisfied the group wasn't following them.

"Well, that was quite exciting." Moistening her lips, Martha placed a hand on her chest. "Do you think they'll come back, Angela?"

"I have no idea." Heart still racing, she let out a slow, relieved breath.

The older woman grasped her husband's arm, her face pale and drawn. "I hope to never see them again."

Angela agreed. She'd heard some tribes were peaceful, others hostile. But how did a woman such as her identify which was which?

Lifting the satchel onto the seat, Angela pulled out a dime novel. *Seth Jones, Captives of the Frontier.* Perhaps she'd find answers to some of her questions inside.

Splendor

Midnight, with three more hours to go before Dutch McFarlin, another of Gabe's deputies, relieved Shane. His position on the top balcony of Noah's blacksmith shop was tight. After six hours, any location would wear on a man.

The clear night and almost full moon made it easier to spot travelers coming from the east. Two more lookouts were on watch tonight. One on the top floor of Ruby's Grand Palace, and the other on the roof of the community building.

They'd started the watch schedule within hours of their meeting at Ruby's. Between the deputies and townsfolk who'd volunteered, Shane believed they had a good chance of spotting Sutton and his men. They presumed the gang was headed for Splendor. He prayed they weren't.

Leaning against the door of the apartment above the shop, he lifted the binoculars, sweeping the open space to the east. Nothing caught his attention.

Taking his position three hours earlier, Shane had passed the time thinking about the cabin he'd purchased from Noah. A thirty minute ride from town, with a spectacular view, it was what he'd been hoping to find. Someday, after he married, Shane would add another bedroom for children.

His chest squeezed on the thought. Shane had always expected to marry and have a family long before now. Life had other plans.

Lifting the binoculars, he swept the east again, seeing nothing threatening to the town. Lowering them, Shane considered the single women he believed might make a good wife. All had traveled west hoping to find love and marriage. They were educated and pretty, not afraid of hard work.

Of the three, Carrie, Rose, and Amelia, he thought Carrie might be the best match. A nurse, she worked at the clinic several days a week. He guessed her to be five-foot-six, with a slender body, sun-streaked auburn hair, and sparkling blue eyes. Shane knew she loved to ride and take long walks.

He'd overheard Carrie say she hoped to one day live in a house with enough room for a garden and her own horse. The cabin would be the perfect place for her to fulfill her dreams. She could be the perfect woman for him.

Then why didn't he feel more anticipation about courting her? Shane knew the reason, but refused to give in to a past he could never get back.

Raising the binoculars, he searched east, almost missing a group of riders approaching Splendor. Blinking, he looked again, counting three men. They were too far away to recognize faces or any other identifying mark.

Rushing down the stairs, he ran to Ruby's and through the back door she'd agreed to keep unlocked. Taking the stairs two at a time, he entered the room where Caleb stood at the window.

"I spotted three riders from the east."

Lowering his binoculars, Caleb's grim expression mirrored Shane's. "I counted three, also. Were you able to identify any of them?"

"No. They're too far away."

Caleb moved toward the door. "Mack's at the community building. I'll alert him while you ride to Gabe's house. I don't want to scare the town by ringing the church bell until we get a better look at them."

Rushing down the stairs to alert the others, a twinge of doubt lodged in Shane's head. Three riders weren't enough for what he believed Sutton intended. Sliding the bridle over his palomino stallion's head, he swung onto the horse's back, not taking the time to cinch up the saddle.

Gabe had built his house a half mile east of town in a clearing surrounded by tall pines. Slowing enough to jump to the ground, Shane pounded on the front door and waited.

Drawing the door open, Gabe stood in the entry wearing pants and nothing else. "What is it?"

"Three riders approaching from the east. Caleb saw them and is letting Mack know. They were too far away to see their faces. I'm guessing they're no more than half a mile out."

"Wake up Cash, Dutch, and Cole." They'd agreed at their meeting if riders approached, the most obvious trail would be from the south end of town. "Take positions as we discussed. We don't want to alert the town until we know who's riding in this late."

Racing back to town, Shane rousted the three deputies out of bed before stopping at the jail to tell Caleb and Mack about Gabe's order. The men moved with speed, taking their positions as Gabe joined them, with Mack staying on the roof of the community building.

"Where are they, Mack?" Gabe pulled his rifle from the scabbard, taking a spot behind the church.

"Maybe two hundred yards out. They've slowed down. Still can't make out anything specific, but they're in no hurry."

Standing at the corner of an unoccupied building at the south end of Palace Street, Shane checked his six-shooter. Satisfied all the chambers were full, he shot quick glances at the other deputies, confirming their locations.

The three riders were outnumbered more than two-to-one. Only fools drew on the lawmen. Then again, there were a lot of fools scattered about the west.

The faint sound of approaching horses had them moving back into the shadows. All except Mack, who lay prone on the roof, his rifle aimed at the trail.

Gabe stepped out from his position as the three ambled along. Raising his rifle, he trained it on the man in front.

"State your business."

Reining to a stop, the three startled as the other deputies made themselves known. Raising their hands in the air, the lead rider urged his horse forward.

"Is this the welcome committee?"

Gabe tucked the rifle tight against his shoulder. "Guess you could say that. What brings you to Splendor at this time of night?"

"Can we lower our hands?"

"Not before answering my question."

"Sheriff Sterling in Big Pine sent us. Said it might be best to ride at night to avoid the renegade Blackfoot in the area."

No one lowered their guns. "Why'd the sheriff send you this way?"

Thinking maybe they'd made a mistake, he assessed their circumstances, knowing he could take down one or two if anyone fired.

"Said you were looking for deputies." His mouth tilted upward. "We're here to apply."

Chapter Seven

The stage entered Big Pine a few hours after sunrise, the four passengers more than ready to stand on solid ground. Stopping in front of an office next door to the livery, the driver jumped down, reaching out a hand to help them to the boardwalk.

"We'll be here three hours. Restaurants are that way." He pointed toward the other end of town. "You can get a bath at the Imperial Hotel. Unless you have clean clothes in your satchels, you'll have to put on the ones you're wearing now." Meaning, he wouldn't be pulling down their luggage from the top of the stage.

Angela ignored the urge to rub her left arm where the bullet entered. The pulsing ache had lessened during the stage ride from Cheyenne. Lifting her arm, she winced at the pain, lowering it before reaching shoulder height.

Martha cringed at the agony on Angela's face. "Maybe we should find a doctor to check your wound?"

"I'd rather get a bath and eat before boarding the stage for Splendor."

"It appears to be two blocks to the Imperial Hotel." Slipping her arm through Angela's good one, Martha looked into the window of each store as they walked to the hotel. "Did you spend much time in Big Pine when you came through with Carson?"

"Two nights. We stayed at the Imperial. You'll love it, Martha. The decorations will remind you of the hotels in Boston. The food at their restaurant is very good."

Martha's stomach growled at the mention of food.

Angela grinned at the color on her friend's face. "We could eat first if you'd like."

"No. I doubt they'd allow us in the dining room with all the dust on our faces. A bath sounds wonderful."

Avoiding wagons and riders, they crossed the street to enter the hotel. Martha looked around, sucking in a breath.

"This is charming. You're right, the decorations are similar to what we'd see in Boston, except on a smaller scale. Oh, there's the dining room." Walking to it, she looked around, seeing a few diners.

"Would you care to see what we're serving today?"

Martha whirled to see a young man holding out a handwritten menu. "Why, yes. Thank you."

"Do you ladies need rooms for tonight?"

Angela joined them, glancing at the paper in Martha's hand. "We came in on the stage. It leaves in less than three hours."

"And you'd like baths?"

"Yes, we would. We'll eat at the restaurant when we're finished."

"I'll order them for you. It will take several minutes. Would you like tea while you wait?" The young man took the menu Martha held out for him.

A slow grin brightened Angela's face. "Tea would be wonderful. Thank you."

"I'll serve it to you in the parlor." He nodded toward a room opposite the dining room before disappearing down a hallway.

Walking to the front window of the parlor, Angela clasped her hands together, watching the activity outside. There was little difference between now and when she'd stayed here with Carson.

The jail was down the street, a bank nearby, and a couple small cafés in between. They'd had breakfast in one of them, finding the food delicious. Ready to turn away, she hesitated, spotting six riders entering the main street from the east.

Their appearance had her breath catching. All were young, wore six-shooters around their waists, expressions severe as their gazes darted around.

She didn't recognize any of them, although warning bells sounded in her head. Whirling around, she hurried to the young man handing a key to the couple at the front desk.

"Your tea should be ready soon."

Angela waved him off. "I'm hoping you can identify a group of men riding down the street." Without waiting for a response, she dashed to the front door, stepping onto the boardwalk. The clerk stood beside her. "Those six men approaching the hotel. Do you recognize any of them?"

Squinting his eyes, he studied them before shaking his head. "I'm sorry, but no. I've never seen any of them."

His answer didn't reassure her. "Thank you." Angela followed him inside, seeing Martha sitting on a sofa in the parlor, a tray with a teapot and cups in front of her.

"Is everything all right?"

"Everything is fine." Not at all sure it was the truth.

Before Martha could pour their tea, the clerk joined them. "Your baths are ready. I'll take your tea to the attendant." Picking up the tray, he nodded toward a hallway. "The women's bathhouse is this way."

Following, Angela couldn't stop herself from glancing over her shoulder.

Splendor

"Right on time." Gabe stood, reaching out his hand to each of the three men.

Their explanations when arriving had been short. Sheriff Parker Sterling in Big Pine encouraged them to talk with Gabe. He'd asked if they had experience. Getting *yes* answers, he'd sent the deputies home, and put the three men up in the apartment at Noah's livery, setting a time to meet at eleven in the morning.

Taking Gabe's hand, the first one introduced himself. "Morgan Wheeler, Sheriff."

The other two introduced themselves as Jonas Taylor and Tucker Nolan.

"Sit down and tell me about your experience. I'd better warn you, I'm not looking for men who'll be here a couple months and move on."

"Fair enough." Jonas pulled up a chair, as did his partners.

"Why don't you start, Jonas? Where you're from, your experience, what brings you to the Montana territory."

"I'm from Indiana. Joined the Union Army near the end of the war. That's when I met Morgan and Tucker. None of us wanted to go back home when the war ended, so we traveled around, ending up in St. Louis. They were short deputies. We applied and were hired. After a couple years, we moved down to Austin to become Texas Rangers. Heckuva job. Those rangers work hard and play harder. We stayed until last year and rode west, then north. Ended up in Big Pine."

Gabe looked at the others, amusement in his eyes. "Same experience with you two?"

"Yes, sir. Except I'm from West Ohio." Morgan looked at Tucker.

"Same as Jonas, I'm from Indiana."

"And all three of you were Texas Rangers?"

Tucker glanced at the others before answering. "Yes, sir. You can send a telegram to Captain Jones in Austin. He'll tell you all about our time with the Rangers."

"May just do that. It's a wonder the three of you stayed together." Gaze narrowing, Gabe waited to see which one of them spoke first. It didn't surprise him it was Morgan, the apparent leader.

"Not if you knew our history."

Leaning back in the chair, Gabe steepled his hands under his chin. "Take as much time as you need, Morgan."

"Dammit, stop your drinking and tell me what you found out." Rand's patience continued to disintegrate as the time with his band of morons wore on. If he didn't need them to go after the deputy, he'd shoot every last one of them.

"You want to hit the bank in Big Pine, boss? I'd say let's do it." The loudest and most brash of the group took one more swallow of whiskey before passing the bottle to another man.

Stalking the short distance to the wide-eyed outlaw, Rand grabbed the bottle, slamming it to the ground. Head rising to stare at the men he'd counted on to kill the deputy, he regretted getting involved with any of them.

Drawing his gun, Rand pointed the weapon at the most obnoxious of the group. "You aren't going to live to do any robbing if you don't stop drinking and give me what I need. You understand?" When the young man didn't answer fast enough, Sutton fired at the ground, inches from his booted feet. Voices lowering, he took a step closer. "Do you understand?"

Giving a brisk nod, the outlaw took several steps away. "Sure, boss. I understand."

Not holstering his gun, Rand crossed the space, staring at each man as he passed. If he didn't get his temper under control, he swore to God he'd kill one of them. Maybe more. The thought intrigued him.

Out of all of them, three had potential, were good shots, with an even temper. The rest were expendable, men the world wouldn't miss. A feral grin tipped the corners of his mouth. Before doing anything he'd regret, he had to get the information out of them.

Pointing the gun at one of the more dependable men who'd ridden in Big Pine, he lifted his chin. "What'd you find out?" Rand couldn't help thinking how he looked ten years old, instead of the seventeen he swore to.

Clearing his throat, the young outlaw stepped forward. "Parker Sterling is the sheriff. A bartender told me there are thirteen deputies. All but a couple dedicated to their job. There are two banks, the biggest being the Territorial Bank of Montana. I didn't ask the bartender more 'cause he started looking at me funny-like. Downed my whiskey and left." Swallowing, he caught looks from the others, including the loudmouth who'd almost gotten them thrown into jail.

"The Territorial Bank might be the best to rob, boss."

"Why's that?"

"It sits at one end of town, separated from other buildings, and a good distance from the jail. We could hit it and ride east without anyone knowing we were there. Well, except for those in the bank." He glanced at his boots, not wanting to say anything to anger Rand. "I think five men could do it. If there are more, we'd risk someone spotting us and going to the sheriff."

Rand rubbed the lengthening growth on his jaw and chin. "Five men, huh? You sure about that?"

"Six at most. And we shouldn't ride in together. Pick a spot and we'll meet at a certain time, rob the bank, and ride out. No dynamite to alert people in town. Instead, we force the bank manager to open the safe."

"How do you propose to get the manager to help?" Rand knew the answer, but he needed to hear it from the kid's mouth.

"Have a gun to his head and another pointed at one of his clerks. He doesn't cooperate, they both die. Her first." The young outlaw didn't even flinch at what he proposed. To a man, the group believed the money was owed to them, and they'd do whatever was required to get it.

His time outlawing told Rand nothing was that easy. Still, the plan was simple and quick—as long as the bank manager didn't do something stupid.

There were two problems with the plan, and those were standing a few feet away. Lifting his gun, he fired two shots, solving both problems.

Chapter Eight

The stage left for Splendor three hours after pulling into Big Pine. The baths and meals had done wonders for Angela and Martha, restoring their energy and good humor.

A few short miles now separated Angela from the man she hoped still lived in Splendor. She'd been a fool not to stay after Carson's death. But her duty had been to Edith, a woman who'd lost both her husband and son in a short period of time.

Another thought occurred to her, one which hadn't come to mind until now. What if he was courting another woman, or had married during the short time she'd been back in Boston?

Placing a hand over her stomach, she pressed, trying to relieve the pain ripping through her. He'd always been handsome, drawing the attention of young and old women alike. Taller, and muscled in a way he hadn't been as a younger man, Shane took her breath away. Age had been good to him.

It had been obvious how much the people in Splendor respected him. The years hadn't taken away his kind nature, his dedication to whatever task he took on. Being a deputy suited him. He'd always reached out to those in need, most taking him up on any kindness. Some, however, could never get past his mixed heritage.

The combination of Irish, Cherokee, and Spanish bestowed him with warm, golden skin, his father's dark auburn hair, and his mother's green eyes. His hair was longer than when he was younger.

Angela hadn't needed to ask anyone his age. She knew he was twenty-eight, six years older than when he'd asked her to marry him. Six years since her father declared he'd never bless a marriage to a breed. She'd heard the word before, always spoken with a good measure of loathing.

Within days of him asking Angela's father for her hand in marriage, she'd been on a train to Boston, sent far away from the man she'd loved since childhood. Six years later, Angela would take a chance she would have never considered in the past.

"Splendor up ahead!"

Stiffening at the driver's words, she laced her fingers together, tightening her grip until the knuckles turned white. Angela tried to remember what she'd planned to say. She'd been practicing all the way from Boston, discarding some ideas while keeping others.

Feeling the stage slow down, she looked out the window, her gaze landing on the large, white church and St. James Hotel several yards away. The stage depot was at the end of the next block, near the livery and telegraph office.

Inhaling a slow breath, letting it out at the same rate, she forced herself to relax. Martha's hand touched her arm.

"Whatever you're nervous about, it will all be fine, Angela. You'll be fine. If you ever want to talk, I'm a good listener."

A smile began to form, but it wouldn't hold. The thought he might reject her, that she'd traveled all this way for nothing, scared her the most. It had been so long, and they'd both changed. Before leaving Boston, Angela had promised herself no matter the risk to her heart, she'd get answers before leaving Splendor.

Leaning against a post outside the jail, Shane watched as the stage came to a stop at the livery. He'd spent the afternoon showing the three new deputies around town, introducing them to anyone they encountered, plus stopping at most businesses.

Shane found them interested in the town, asking intelligent questions, ones he'd expect from experienced lawmen. Their last stop was the house Noah selected for them. Furnished, with two bedrooms, three stoves, and plenty of room. The town would pay for it, but they'd have to figure out the sleeping arrangements themselves.

Shoving away from the post, Shane wanted nothing more than a beer, hot bath, and bed. The last few days had been long, and he didn't expect much to change until Sutton showed himself.

His gaze moved down the boardwalk toward the stage, watching as the driver helped a young woman to the ground. A moment passed before the driver helped another woman down. Smoothing her shirt, she adjusted her hat before turning in his direction.

Jaw dropping, Shane stopped, his body rigid. Forcing air in and out of his lungs, he took a few tentative steps forward, not believing what his eyes confirmed. Getting within a few feet of the woman, his hands clenched at his sides.

"Hello, Shane." Her soft voice was tentative as her gaze searched his.

"What are you doing here, Angela?" His harsh words had her taking a step back.

"I... Well, I..." She couldn't seem to get the rest out.

Observing from a few feet away, Martha moved to Angela's side. "I'm Miss Martha van Plew, and you are?"

Shane wanted to forget his manners and ignore the woman. Touching the brim of his hat, his expression still steeped in anger, he focused on her. "I'm Deputy Shane Banderas." Having done his duty, he turned back to Angela, arms crossed. "Why are you here?"

Her hesitant smile faltered at what she took to be revulsion on his face. Before she could respond, Jonas Taylor, one of the new deputies, stopped next to Shane.

"Do you women need help to the hotel?"

Shane sent Jonas a withering look before Martha spoke. "Thank you, Deputy. I'm Miss Martha van Plew, and this is Miss Angela Baldwin. We traveled here from Boston. We're staying at the St. James Hotel." Taking Angela's arm, she propelled her friend around Shane.

"You want to help with the bags, Shane?"

Gaze boring into Angela's back, he shook his head. "Nope. You're doing just fine."

Surprised, but unperturbed, Jonas shrugged. Grabbing their three bags, he followed the women to the St. James.

Arms still crossed, Shane watched them march up the street, Martha chattering to Jonas, who nodded every few seconds. He would've laughed if he wasn't still stunned to see Angela back in Splendor.

After Carson's death, they'd spoken little before she'd boarded the stagecoach for the return trip to Boston. It had been a clear sign she had no desire to explore a future with him.

Shane didn't know why it hurt to know she could leave him behind for a second time. His brain told him he shouldn't have expected her to stay after the death of her fiancé. She had obligations in Boston, a grieving mother to support. Selfish as it was, his heart disagreed.

Refusing to waste more time on questioning the past, he continued past the telegraph office to the livery. He and Noah still had details to agree on before Shane took possession of the cabin. Thirty minutes up the mountain by horseback, it was close to town while giving him the space he craved.

"Deputy Banderas!"

Turning, a smile altered his features at the sight of Carrie Galloway rushing toward him. He'd settled on her as a woman to learn more about. Noting her severe expression, he crossed the distance to her.

"What's wrong?"

"It's Enoch Weaver. He collapsed." She whirled to point at a crumpled figure not far from the lumber yard. "I can't lift him."

Leaving her behind, he ran toward the man all the deputies liked and respected. Considered the town drunk by many, they knew him to be a well-educated lawyer who'd left his lucrative practice in Cincinnati after the tragic deaths of his wife and son. It had been their good fortune he'd landed in Splendor.

Dropping beside him, Shane felt for a pulse. "Enoch, can you hear me?"

Carrie knelt next to him. "He's still breathing."

Shane leaned down next to Enoch's ear. "Enoch." At no response, he slid his arms underneath, stood, and hurried to the clinic.

Not a big man, Enoch was still heavy in his arms. Reaching the clinic, Shane's breath came in gasps as he took the steps up to the door. Skirting around him, Carrie shoved the door open.

"Take him in the examination room to the right. I'll get the doctor."

Laying him on the bed, Shane continued to say Enoch's name over and over, hoping for a response. His friend remained silent.

Doctor Clay McCord joined Shane, moving to the other side of the bed. "Carrie and I will take over, Shane.

Do you want to wait, or should I send word of his condition?"

"I'll wait."

Removing his hat, he set it on a chair in the waiting room, taking a seat beside it. Closing his eyes, he massaged the back of his neck, thinking of the older man. Enoch had suffered what the doctor decided was a heart attack several months earlier, recovering after a few days.

Leaning his head against the wall, Shane wondered how many such episodes a body could take. Including a body soaked in alcohol after the deaths of Enoch's wife and son. He'd sobered over time, still presenting himself to most of the townsfolk in order to watch the happenings in town, and report anything suspicious to Gabe or one of the deputies.

Shane hadn't realized he'd fallen asleep until a light hand on his shoulder shook him awake. Blinking, he rubbed his eyes, remembering where he was and why. Sitting up, he stood to face Doc McCord.

"How is Enoch?"

"Asleep. This attack was worse than his first one. To be honest, he's older and not in good shape. I don't know if he'll recover. I'll be keeping him at the clinic so Doc Worthington and I can watch him."

"What about when he goes home?"

Placing a hand on Shane's shoulder, the doctor's lips pressed into a hard line. "Let's focus on his recovery here before worrying about anything else."

The meaning was clear. No use planning for the future when there may not be one. Giving a slow nod, Shane retrieved his hat.

"Thanks, Doc. I'd better let Gabe know what happened. I'll be back in the morning."

The late afternoon breeze wrapped around him as he crossed the distance between the clinic and jail. Walking past Ruby's Grand Palace, hearing the music, he couldn't work up the enthusiasm to stop for a drink.

On normal days, he'd stop at the Dixie, Wild Rose, or Ruby's for a whiskey before returning home. Today hadn't been normal. He'd made his rounds with the three new deputies. At the time, he didn't realize it would be the one good part of the day.

Seeing Angela step off the stage had stunned him. Shane had never thought he'd see her again, didn't want to see her again. He'd created a new future in his mind, one which included someone else, not the woman who'd said she loved him, then disappeared. She'd known where he lived, knew his address. Yet, in all those years, she'd never tried to get a letter to him.

Showing up in Splendor months ago with her fiancé had caused the old pain to return. He'd thought any leftover feelings for his first love were long buried. Seeing her with Carson, her arm through his, confirmed how much he still loved Angela.

Shane didn't know what to make of her showing up a second time in Splendor. In truth, he didn't care. Or didn't want to care. Their lives had changed a great deal in six years. What he wanted at twenty-two, with little life experience, bared no resemblance to what he wanted now.

Angela Baldwin, the woman she'd become, would not play a part in his future.

Chapter Nine

Angela's eyes popped open, closing tight at the bright morning sun streaming through the lace curtains. It took a moment for her to remember where she was, and why. Her stomach clenched at Shane's reaction to seeing her, his cold demeanor and hateful gaze.

For a brief moment, she thought of continuing their journey to San Francisco, doing her best to forget all about the lawman. Grimacing, she discarded the idea. Angela had already made too many mistakes with Shane, she refused to make another. Hightailing it out of Splendor would solve nothing.

Determined to start today with determination and a new sense of purpose, she slid her feet to the ground. It didn't take long to finish her ablutions and dress. Taking a last look in the mirror, she clutched her reticule and knocked on the room next door. Martha drew it open, dressed for the day.

"Are you ready to see the town?"

"Oh, yes. Shall we start with breakfast?"

Angela couldn't stop herself from smiling at Martha's enthusiasm. Throughout the trip, she'd never lost her optimistic attitude, hadn't complained once, and looked forward to each day. Angela wished she felt the same.

Shane's reaction yesterday forced her to change her course of action. She'd never thought he'd accept her with open arms. The open hostility had been a surprise. It hurt, but she understood. Instead of long walks, horseback rides, and meals to see if they could still suit, she'd have to take a different approach.

Entering the Eagle's Nest on the first floor of the hotel, Thomas rushed toward them. Angela had heard he'd been with the hotel and restaurant since they'd opened. He had been off when they arrived the day before.

"Miss Baldwin. I'm glad to see you back in Splendor. Will you be eating breakfast with us?"

"Yes, Thomas. This is Miss van Plew, a good friend of mine."

Giving a slight nod, he motioned them to a table by the front window. "Will this be all right?"

"Perfect," Martha answered. Handing them menus, he took their orders before leaving them alone. Looking around the spacious dining room, she settled her gaze back on Angela. "This is beautiful."

"I thought the same when Carson and I arrived. The food is good, and Thomas is quite accommodating." Angela's attention was drawn outside at shouts loud enough to be heard through the windows.

Two men faced each other in the middle of the street. She couldn't hear their words, but she could see hands hovering over their six-shooters.

From the corner of her eyes, she watched as another man approached, a badge visible on his shirt. Another deputy came toward them, her breath hitching when her gaze moved to his face.

Shane.

"Isn't that the man you spoke to after we arrived?"

Angela heard Martha's question, but the answer wouldn't come as the scene played out before her. Shane put a hand on one man's shoulder, saying something she couldn't hear. The other deputy did the same with the other man. She couldn't draw a full breath, her heart pounding in her chest.

Unable to move from her spot in the dining room, her fear receded when Shane led one man to the boardwalk while his partner took the other to the opposite side of the street. Letting out a shaky breath, Angela shifted to look at Martha, who appeared pale.

"Are you feeling all right?"

Touching her face with a handkerchief, Martha nodded. "That was, well...exciting. For a moment, I thought someone would be shot."

"Yes, so did I." Picking up a fork, she scooped a small amount of eggs, sliding them into her mouth. Chewing, she once again glanced out the window.

Shane still stood across the street, talking with one of the two men. When they parted, he lifted his head to look around, his gaze landing on her. Heart fluttering, Angela found she couldn't look away. Staring at each other for long moments, Shane's features didn't change as another man stopped beside him.

The moment lost, she focused back on her plate of food. The eggs and bacon no longer appealed. Setting down her fork, she sipped coffee, hoping her appetite would return.

Finishing her breakfast, Martha touched the corners of her mouth with a napkin before leaning forward. "You must tell me why you and the deputy are at odds."

She'd expected her friend's curiosity. Sighing, she set her napkin on the table. "Shane and I knew each other when we were children."

Ignoring Martha's intake of breath, she went on to explain their plans to marry before her father sent her to Boston. "We never saw each other again before Carson brought me west. Shane never knew where I'd gone."

"Couldn't you have written him?"

"I did try, but Mr. Winslow insisted any correspondence be approved by him. Needless to say, he destroyed my letter to Shane. I didn't know this until after his death. By then, it was assumed Carson and I would marry."

Dabbing at a tear at the corner of her eye, Martha shook her head. "Two star-crossed lovers meeting all those years later in a frontier town. It's so romantic."

Choking out a scornful laugh, Angela stared down at her lap. "I should've tried harder to get a letter to Shane."

"You *must* explain it to him. I'm sure he'll be moved by what you have to say."

Somehow, Angela didn't believe the same. "I hope to get him alone long enough to do just that. After the way he acted yesterday, I have my doubts he'll spare me the time."

Making a sound of frustration, Martha's gaze narrowed on hers. "Then we'll have to persuade him it's in his best interest to listen to your explanation."

Angela agreed, but getting the stubborn lawman to listen wouldn't be easy.

~~~

Shane slammed the door to the jail open, wincing when Gabe looked up, a brow raised. "Sorry."

Gabe's mouth twitched at the corners. "Already having a bad day?"

Muttering a curse, Shane shook his head, noting other than him and Gabe, the jail was empty. Lowering himself into a chair, he leaned back.

"Everything is fine. Broke up a fight between two men over a woman. Hawke took one and I took the other. Seems the one Hawke spoke with is the husband. He'd packed up his family and was leaving the area. Turns out his wife was married to the other man before her current husband."

Rubbing his temples, Shane had no intention of discussing the real reason for his short temper. Seeing Angela through the window of the Eagle's Nest soured his mood. He'd spent the night figuring out how to start courting Carrie. He now realized any attempt to get to know the enticing woman would have to wait until he settled his past with Angela.

"According to the schedule, you're on watch at the top floor of the St. James today."

Shane nodded, saying nothing, his thoughts back on Angela.

"Hawke will replace you at six, after he and Beauty have had their supper."

Again, he nodded, lost in the image of Angela sitting in the restaurant.

Gabe stood, walking around his desk to stand in front of Shane. Snapping his fingers, his deputy jerked.

"Sorry, Gabe. What did you say?"

Chuckling, Gabe leaned a hip against his desk, crossing his arms. "I'm here if you ever want to talk."

"Thanks, but I'll be all right. There's a few things I have to work out, but nothing will affect my job."

"Fair enough. Eat lunch, then get to your post at the hotel. Sterling sent word no one had spotted Sutton and his men. Could be a good sign."

"Might mean he's skipping Big Pine and coming straight here." Shane thought of the possible deaths if Sutton rode into town without anyone spotting him. "We have to stop him before he reaches Splendor."

"Easy to say. Hard to do."

Scooting his chair back, Shane stood. "Nothing's impossible."

Straightening, Gabe returned to his chair. "True. Think about how you propose to stop them, and we'll get with the others to talk about details. Now, get out of here."

Crossing the street to the boardinghouse restaurant, Shane scanned the room before sitting down. He wasn't ready to face Angela again. The way he'd handled her arrival yesterday was wrong. There were a hundred things he could've done without exhibiting his anger to those within earshot.

The contempt on her friend's face, Jonas jumping in to calm the situation, still ate at him. Shane was known for his calm in tense conditions. No one could prove it by his reaction when Angela departed the stage.

Across the room, the three new deputies motioned him to their table. Preferring a table alone, he accepted their invitation, taking a seat with a view toward the school.

"How you boys doing today?"

"Making rounds, Shane. Getting to know the people." Tucker sipped his coffee. "Seems like a real nice town."

"Splendor is bigger than we thought." Jonas quieted when Suzanne placed plates in front of them.

"What'll you have, Shane?"

"Meatloaf and potatoes, Suzanne. Do you have pie today?"

"Apple, berry, and peach."

"Save me a slice of peach. Is Nick back in town?"

Nodding, she shot a look out the window. "Um...yes. He got back late last night. Do you know those women?"

Following her gaze, he grimaced. "They came in on yesterday's stage."

"The one with blonde hair looks familiar."

Shane continued watching as the women walked past the schoolhouse toward the creek. "Do you remember Carson Winslow?"

"Sure. He was... Wait. That's the fiancée. Such a horrible tragedy. Wonder what brought her back to Splendor."

Jonas, Tucker, and Morgan kept quiet, listening to the exchange. Jonas had shared with them what he saw when the women got off the stage, including Shane's reaction to the blonde. Suzanne's comments made them even more curious about what Jonas witnessed.

"I don't know why she came back, Suzanne. Maybe this is a stop on her way to San Francisco. Someone as citified as her would never make a home in Splendor."

Laughing, Suzanne chucked him on the chin. "Tell the same to Caro, Isabella, and Rachel. But be prepared for an argument. I'll get your lunch."

Rubbing his brow, Shane considered her words. Those women had come from privilege, yet each had taken little time adjusting to Splendor.

Could Angela be considering starting a new life here? And if so, why?

Chapter Ten

Shane paced the top floor balcony of the St. James, watching for Sutton while considering the possibility Angela may have chosen Splendor as her new home. The notion was hard to accept.

"Why now?" Shane grumbled, continuing to pace.

It had taken years to make the decision to move on with his life, selecting a woman he intended to marry, and buy a home for his future family. Carrie matched what he expected in a wife. Her caring nature would make her a wonderful mother, and in time, he hoped to fall in love with her, and she him.

Picking up the binoculars, he scanned the east, the same as Dutch would be doing above the livery, and Hawke on the top floor of Ruby's. Disappointed at no sign of the outlaws, he lowered them to resume his pacing.

Shane thought Angela believed they could resume their relationship as if six years hadn't passed, as if she hadn't accepted another man's proposal to marry. He didn't know Carrie's background, but he knew a great deal about Angela's.

Her father had let Shane believe Angela had died. The lie became apparent years later when she'd arrived in Splendor with her fiancé, Carson Winslow. Since then, Shane's thoughts had shifted between trying to forget her and wondering why she'd never tried to contact him.

She hadn't tried to reach him by letter or telegram. Angela had forgotten him as easily as she'd allowed her father to send her away.

Reminding himself of the past made it easier to let his mind focus on Carrie. Resting his hands on the handrail, he looked down, letting out a sigh. Angela and Martha walked along the creek, stopping every few feet to toss a rock in the water or admire one of the many wildflowers growing along the shoreline.

Before he could step away, a genuine laugh drifted up to him. Angela's laugh when something amused her. The sound threw him back years to a place he didn't want to be. Shane believed the past should stay there, and not intrude on present day life.

Instead of moving away, he continued to stare down at her, heart thudding in his chest. Cursing under his breath, he whirled around, crossing the short distance to the door of the room Thomas had given the deputies while watching for the outlaws.

Inside, a coffeepot sat on a stove, along with a nearby tray of cups and sugar. Porcelain cups and saucers from the Eagle's Nest. Shane chuckled at the sight. Filling a cup, he took a sip, letting the warm liquid flow down his throat to calm his stomach.

Knowing he had to return to the balcony, he swallowed the last of the coffee, resuming his position outside. Angela and Martha were nowhere in sight, which suited him fine.

Using the binoculars, he spotted the afternoon stage from Big Pine. Unless the outlaws were passengers, his instincts told him they wouldn't be riding in today. Tonight, maybe, but not while the sun shone on Splendor.

"The stage has arrived, Angela. Let's see who gets off." From their table, Martha turned the chair toward the window.

They'd stopped at the boardinghouse restaurant for coffee and pie before talking to Noah Brandt about renting two horses for a short ride outside of town. Angela had ridden a couple times after Carson went missing. Gabe had insisted a deputy accompany her, which was more than she'd expected from a sheriff who didn't know her. Even with an escort, she found the time on the back of a horse helped lessen her fear about her fiancé.

Angela hoped today's ride would allow her to relax, and consider the best way to approach Shane. The enthusiasm she had during the trip west had faltered at her initial encounter with him. Locking gazes on each other this morning hadn't been any better.

Following the direction of Martha's gaze, Angela noticed two cowboys step to the ground. She saw nothing intriguing about either of them, including the six-shooters hung low on their hips.

Losing interest, she took another bite of berry pie, her thoughts returning to Shane. He'd made it obvious he had no feelings for her, except revulsion. Hate would be too strong. Dislike not strong enough. Shane didn't have to say the words to know he didn't want her in Splendor, would be happy to see her board the next stage and leave.

"We don't have to stay here, Angela."

Swallowing the bite of pie, she shot a look at Martha. "What do you mean?"

"It's obvious how the deputy's dismissal hurts you. Why stay and allow him to cause you pain? We can leave, take the stage back to Cheyenne, then catch the train to San Francisco. I've been told it's a magnificent trip. Who knows? You might meet the perfect man on our travels."

Stirring sugar into her coffee, Angela made no reaction to the suggestion. She'd already met the perfect man, long ago as a young girl, and lost him.

"Angela?"

"Yes?"

"Did you even hear what I said?"

She did, but had no idea how to respond. "I'm sorry, what did you say?"

Martha repeated her idea, embellishing a little bit more this time. "So, what do you think?"

"I appreciate your concern, but I'll be fine. Besides, there are so many places you should see before we leave. Let's stay at least a week, then decide."

"As long as you're certain. I'll stay as long as you'd like."

Boots pounding on the plank floor drew their attention to the two cowboys who'd arrived on the stage.

Getting a closer look at them, Angela guessed them to be younger than Martha, instead of older, as she'd first thought.

The men's gazes darted about the restaurant, as if looking for something, or someone. Taking a table across the room, they ordered before lowering their heads to talk.

"Are you ready to talk to Mr. Brandt?" Martha finished the last of the coffee, setting her cup aside.

Drawing in a breath, she blew it out. "Yes. Let's go."

Stepping outside, Angela noticed the increase in number of wagons and people on the boardwalk. Adjusting her bonnet, she led the way to the livery.

Noah stood at the counter of his saddlery and tack shop. Angela hadn't noticed the mining supplies against one wall when she'd been inside before, instead focusing on the beautiful leather work. He lifted his head from what he was doing, a grin forming on his face.

"I heard you were back in town, Miss Baldwin. It's good to see you."

"You also, Mr. Brandt. This is my good friend, Miss Martha van Plew."

"It's a pleasure, Miss van Plew. Have you enjoyed your trip so far?"

"I have. Splendor is charming, and the hotel is so much more than I expected."

Chuckling, Noah walked around the counter. "Gabe was interested in his uncle's businesses since we were children. We even worked in one of the hotels while growing up."

Angela's brow lifted. "You've known each other a long time."

"Most of our lives. My father worked for Gabe's, although we weren't in the same social position as the Evans family. We joined the Union Army together, and came west when the war ended. So, what can I do for you?"

"We want to rent horses for the afternoon. I recall a trail you recommended on my last trip. Martha would love it."

Noah's expression shifted to a frown. "I'm afraid it's not a good idea, ladies."

Matching his frown, Angela cocked her head to the side. "Why?"

"We've got some trouble coming our way. No one knows when it will get here, but it's not safe for women to ride outside the town limits."

Noah looked up at the same time the women turned toward the sound of someone entering. "Shane. What can I do for you?"

Ignoring Noah's question, his gaze bored into Angela. "What are you doing here?" His voice was the same as the day before. Hard, unyielding, accusatory.

Squaring her shoulders, she lifted her chin. "Not that it's your business, but we're here to rent horses for the afternoon."

"No."

Blinking, her eyes narrowed on his. "No?"

Crossing his arms, he glared at her. "You heard me."

"This is not your decision. It's ours."

"Is that so? Noah, you plan on setting up these women with horses?"

Leaning against the counter, he shook his head. "I already told them we've got trouble coming."

"Noah's right. Everyone knows to stay close to town, and be watching for anything suspicious."

Matching his stance, she crossed her arms. "Well, we hadn't heard anything about it until Mr. Brandt told us. I still believe you're overreacting. There must be someone who'll rent us horses."

Smirking, Shane shook his head. "Afraid not. No one would be foolish enough, not with what's coming our way." Opening the door, he motioned toward the outside. "Might as well find something else to occupy your time. Maybe you could find a man to spend time with, Angie."

Feeling heat creep up her face, she closed the distance between them. Without hesitating, she raised her hand. Before Shane knew what to expect, a harsh slap snapped his head to the side.

"What the hell..."

"Age hasn't been your friend, Shane Banderas. You've turned into a nasty, venomous man I don't recognize." Hands fisting at her sides, her body began to shake. "I came to Splendor because of you, but now realize my efforts were wasted."

Stilling at her words, he recovered to lean down within inches of her face. "Then leave."

"Ha! You'd like that, wouldn't you? Well, too bad. Martha and I plan to stay for a good, long time. In fact, I heard Mr. Brandt has houses he rents." Tearing her gaze away, she looked at Noah. "Is that true?"

Clearing his throat, he grimaced at the sudden change. "Ma'am, I don't—"

"Don't you dare treat me as if I'm some addled headed woman. Do you, or do you not, rent your houses?"

Huffing out a breath, Noah shot Shane an apologetic look. "Yes, ma'am, I do. What do you need?"

"Two bedrooms. Do you have one available?"

Knowing his friend wouldn't lie, Shane's jaw clenched. "Yes. There's a two bedroom real close to here. It's next door to Deputy Dutch McFarlin. It's already got furniture. You'll need to buy kitchen goods and whatever linens you need."

"Excellent. I'll take it." Angela reached into her reticule, taking out a pouch. "What do I owe you for the first month?"

Mentioning a price, she counted out the money, handing it to him.

"Would you mind showing it to us? I'd like to move in our belongings as soon as possible."

Unable to keep quiet, Shane gripped her shoulders. "You are not staying in Splendor, Angie."

"Again, it is none of your business." She returned her attention to Noah. "Well?"

Shane tried again. "Doesn't it matter that you aren't welcome here?"

"From what I've seen and the people we've met, I believe there is just one person who doesn't want us here. It's a shame he doesn't have a say."

Running a hand through his hair, a growl emanated from his throat. "What will you do? You have no skills, no way to make a living. You know nothing of life in Montana or the dangers all around us. You aren't built for a life such as this. Hard work and harsh conditions. You won't last six months."

Martha, who'd remained silent, groaned, knowing how Angela would respond. Clenching her hands together, she waited for the expected response.

Angela's features relaxed, a wicked gleam in her eyes. "You know nothing about me, Shane. I've learned a great deal in six years, lost even more. Hard work does not scare me. Neither do loathsome men who assume they know what's best for me." Lifting her hand, she poked a finger at his chest. "My life with the Winslows was not all social functions and trips to the salon. There was much more going on inside that home. All you need to know is you're not running me out of Splendor. This is now my home, and I'll be darned if we'll leave because of you." Whirling around, she nodded at Noah. "Martha and I are ready for you to show us our new home."

Chapter Eleven

Mouth slack, Shane watched Angela and Martha march out of the saddlery. Noah followed a moment later, holding a key to the house in his hand.

"Miss Baldwin has a whole lot of sass. Still, I'm thinking you were pretty hard on her, Shane. I've never seen you act that way toward a woman."

Rubbing his jaw, Shane fell in step beside Noah. "She shouldn't be here."

"Yeah, your thoughts were real clear. So were hers. How long have you known her?"

"Too darn long." Seeing the women slow down, he lowered his voice. "Since we were children. She hasn't changed." It was a lie. Angela had changed a great deal since leaving him behind.

Vivacious, with a quick smile and kind word for everyone, Angela had made friends with little ease. She rode her old mare almost every day, helped her mother in the house, and spent any free time reading or with Shane. Not pampered, but also not interested in the hard work associated with a farm.

"Angela left our hometown for Boston at eighteen. She lived with the Winslows for six years, one of the wealthiest families in the city. I doubt she knows anything about splitting wood for the cold season, cooking, washing, or cleaning. The family had help for those chores. Trust me, she'll be on her way back to Boston within three months, maybe sooner."

"Guess we'll see if you're right." Reaching the women, Noah pointed to a house next to Dutch's. "Built this block a couple years ago. Most of the houses are taken. I'll show you the inside."

Angela shot Shane a withering glance. "What are you doing here?"

Shrugging, a small smile tugged at the corners of his mouth. "Curious to see which house will have a short-term tenant."

Refusing to be dragged back into an argument, she followed Noah. Pushing the door open, he stepped aside for her and Martha to enter. Staying on the stoop, he leaned against the post.

"Something tells me once she makes up her mind, little will change it."

Shane agreed, wishing he'd remembered her stubborn streak. It had been endearing when they were young.

"It's quite suitable, Mr. Brandt. We'll move our belongings later today. Thank you for taking the time to show it to us." Leaving the men behind, she and Martha headed in the direction of the St. James.

"Are you going to offer your help to move them over?" Noah's eyes crinkled with amusement.

"The house is their decision. I've got other work to do. Say hello to your beautiful wife for me."

Noah waited until Shane disappeared around the corner of the telegraph office before throwing back his head to laugh.

"What were you thinking, Angela? We never discussed staying in Splendor for months. A few weeks, yes, but months?" Simmering with frustration, Martha folded her clothes, placing them in her open luggage. "I don't think I have enough funds to stay here so long, then travel to San Francisco."

Angela sat on the edge of her friend's bed, lowering her face into her hands. "I don't know why I had such a strong reaction to Shane ordering me to leave. He never acted this way when we were younger."

Sitting next to her, Martha patted her arm. "He's angry. At you and the fact you're here in Splendor. You've disrupted his life, and if we stay, he knows you'll interrupt it even more. I can't help wondering if he might be courting someone."

Lifting her head, Angela's eyes grew wide. "What?"

"What if Shane is courting someone? It would explain why he's so determined to see you leave town."

Rising, Angela paced to the window, whirling back toward Martha. "I've never seen him with anyone. I'm certain there wasn't a woman the last time I was here."

"It's been several months since you were in Splendor. He may have met someone during the time you were away." Seeing Angela's distress, Martha added, "I'm not saying he is courting someone, but it's one explanation for his harsh words."

"Yes, it is. One I hadn't given much thought." Continuing to pace, Angela thought of her rash decision to rent a house from Noah.

The rooms were spacious and clean, with stoves in the kitchen and each bedroom. Seeing them earlier, her mind had gone to the work required to live in Montana during the winter. She imagined there were boys who'd split and stack wood for some coin. Cooking and cleaning weren't an issue. She'd done plenty of both in the Winslow household the first two years after arriving.

"Three months."

Martha blinked in confusion. "Three months?"

"We'll stay three months, then discuss staying longer or leaving."

Folding her hands in her lap, Martha stared down at them. "I don't know if I have enough funds to last." Raising her head, she worried her bottom lip. "Assuming we'll still be traveling to San Francisco after the three months."

Guilt wafted through Angela. She hadn't spent any time wondering how the decision to stay would affect Martha. Boarding the train in Boston, the younger woman had been excited beyond reason to travel to the Pacific Ocean. She now believed they might never get there.

"No matter what happens, we will continue our trip, Martha. As for funds, if yours aren't sufficient, I'll provide the difference."

"Papa would never allow that."

Angela's mouth tipped into a grin. "Your father doesn't have to know."

"It's quite hard to keep anything from him." Martha's eyes sparkled with mirth. "But it would be fun trying."

"I may never succeed in getting Shane to hear my side before we leave. Whatever happens between him and me doesn't mean you can't meet someone while we're here. Maybe your perfect man lives within blocks of the hotel."

Unclenching her hands, Martha sat up, her expression brightening. "Or perhaps he'll be a rancher. Maybe I've already seen him on the street. Wouldn't that be incredible?"

Her smile matching Martha's, Angela sat down next to her. "Yes, it would. I've learned you never know when someone special will cross your path. Meaning, you must always be open to meeting new people."

"Perhaps both of us should keep our possibilities open."

Considering how their encounters had gone so far, Martha's idea had merit. "Yes, it may be wise for me to be open, as well as you. Now, let's pack and move our belongings to our new home."

Shane's features darkened, causing him to take another sip of his whiskey. He'd picked the Dixie for a reason. From his spot at the bar, he had a clear view of anyone passing by, including two women with luggage.

Sure enough, he'd been at the bar less than fifteen minutes when they appeared, heads high, followed by two men carrying their belongings. Unlike the irritation he expected, pride and amusement had his mouth twisting into an odd grin. Not a scowl, but not a smile.

"Aren't those the women who came in on the stage?" Nick Barnett, one of the owners of the Dixie, took a spot next to Shane. "Suzanne told me about them. Says one was Carson Winslow's fiancée. Isn't she the blonde?"

"Yeah." Taking another slow sip of whiskey as they disappeared around the corner, he faced the bar. "They've decided to stay for a while. Rented one of Noah's houses."

Hearing the unease in Shane's voice, Nick lifted a brow. "Is that a problem?"

Pausing a moment, he gave a slow shake of his head. "No. How was your trip to Big Pine?"

"Profitable. We'll be opening a saloon there, right next to the Imperial Hotel." Nick glanced at his long time bartender. "Paul may be interested in moving there to bartend and manage the place."

"Paul's a good man, loyal to you and Gabe. He'll be hard to replace."

"Amos Henderson has offered to take Paul's place until we find someone else. He owned the Wild Rose before we bought him out. Seems he's tired of being retired."

Amos had left Splendor after selling the saloon, returning several months earlier. He'd been an unwilling part of the tragedy which left Carson dead.

"He spends a good deal of time helping Silas at the lumber mill."

"Without pay. Not that Amos needs the money, but he'll get paid if he takes over the bar." Nick nodded at Paul, who set a whiskey in front of him. "We plan to open in a month."

Shane tried to keep his mind off Angela as Nick spoke, not succeeding. "Not much time."

"We're taking over an existing bar. It's in decent shape, but some changes will be made. I've already placed an order with our suppliers." Nick nodded toward the girl serving drinks. "We'll have to hire the women. Shouldn't be hard."

Tossing back the last of his whiskey, Shane held out his hand, shaking Nick's. "Let me know if there's anything I can do."

"Thanks for the offer. I'll keep it in mind."

Resisting the urge to pass by Angela's house on the way to his, Shane took a different route home. He'd hoped to be courting Carrie by now. Angela's decision to stay in Splendor forced him to put off those plans.

The disappointment he expected never came. Shane refused to spend time trying to understand his lack of reaction. His lips edged upward, recalling the way she defied him at the saddlery. This side of her was new. She'd been more complacent, shying away from confrontation before leaving for Boston.

Now, Angela stood her ground, defending what she wanted, arguing to get her point across. To be honest, he preferred the new Angela. Courageous and strong, not backing down when faced with Shane's hostility. He'd been angry, but also intrigued.

Stopping at the bottom stairs to his front door, he chanced a look down the street toward Angela's new home. Four houses away. A mere hundred feet separated them, yet the actual gap was much bigger.

Ignoring the disappointment at not seeing her, he bounded up the stairs, shoved open the door, and froze. The hairs on the back of his neck prickled. Someone had been inside.

The jacket he'd hung on a hook now lay in a heap on the floor. The overstuffed chair he'd purchased from Noah was askew, facing the kitchen instead of toward the front window.

Resting a hand on the butt of his gun, he continued into the first bedroom. His bedroom. The pillows were out of place, as were the blankets. The door to the wardrobe was open, when he knew it was closed when he left. Nothing seemed to be missing. Drawing his gun, he held it in front of him.

Moving to the second bedroom, he found nothing had been disturbed other than the wardrobe door standing open. Not a surprise since Hawke had taken all his belongings with him when he'd married Beauty, moving into her house.

Backing out of the room, he spun around, aiming his gun straight ahead. Satisfied no one was still in the house, he lowered his gun before crossing the kitchen to the back door. He found it closed, but not locked. Shane couldn't remember if he'd checked it before leaving that morning.

It wasn't unusual for him to leave his house unlocked. Most in town did the same. Businesses were different. Few would consider offering up their goods to thieves.

Standing in the middle of his living room, he made a slow turn. Other than items being out of place, he was certain nothing had been taken. Any important documents were kept in a special box locked in the vault at the Bank of Splendor. He kept a small amount of money in a pocket, never leaving any at home.

Shane considered who would gain anything by sifting through his belongings. The answer hit him as fast as a bolt of lightning.

Rushing out of the house, he paid no attention to those waving or shouting greetings on his way to the jail.

Chapter Twelve

Martha lifted the cast iron Dutch oven with two hands as if she'd never seen one before. "These are so much heavier than I imagined. Have you ever used one?"

"Many times. It's wonderful for roasts and chicken. We should buy this one and the smaller size. Oh, and we must have a cornbread pan." Angela picked up the cast iron pan with slots for cornbread dough. "Also a griddle and fry pan."

Stan Petermann, the owner of the general store, stood close by, jotting down their selections. "You'll need a few utensils."

"Would you mind selecting them for us? We'll require a mixing bowl and coffeepot, too."

Stan jotted those down, looking up. "Do you need supper plates?"

"Luncheon and supper. And flatware for four."

"Bedsheets?" Stan asked.

"And pillows."

Crossing the street several minutes later, they decided to have supper at the boardinghouse this evening. Tomorrow, they'd cook. Or Angela would, with Martha watching.

Shown to a table at the back with a view of the school, they removed their bonnets, feeling the strain of a long, eventful day. After ordering roast beef with potatoes,

Angela pulled out a piece of paper and pencil she'd purchased at the general store.

Martha cocked a brow. "What are you writing down?"

"Items we still need to purchase. Staples, vegetables, and meat for tomorrow." Her head swiveled at the sound of boots falling on the wood floor. Jaw dropping, she snapped it shut.

"Ladies."

"Good evening, Deputy Banderas." Martha ignored the way Angela's foot collided with her leg. "Please join us for supper."

Removing his hat, he pulled out a chair. "Thank you for the invitation."

One of the servers visited the table, taking his order after setting down a cup of coffee. "Ladies, your meals are almost ready."

"How did your move to the house go?" Sipping his coffee, Shane glanced at Angela over the rim of his cup, amused at her sour expression.

Martha leaned toward him. "Quite well. We came here after ordering a number of items at the general store. Mr. Petermann will deliver our purchases after he finishes supper. Such a nice man."

"He's at least twice your age, Martha," Angela admonished.

"Almost three times," Shane added.

Flushing, Martha glared at both. "You know perfectly well I didn't mean it in that way."

Growing quiet while their meals were served, they ate in silence for several minutes.

"What about you, Deputy? How was your day?"

He watched Angela from the corner of his eye before responding to Martha. "Other than setting off an argument at Noah's, it went well. No arrests, and so far, no fights in the saloons."

Hiding her grin at the mention of their encounter, Angela's brows drew together. "No arrests and fights equal a good day?"

"For most of us, yes. Some of the deputies get bored if there isn't a little action."

"Besides bar brawls, what else saves them from boredom?" Angela sliced a small portion of roast, placing it in her mouth.

"Wives storming into a saloon to drag their husbands away, stealing, bank robbery, rustling, saloon girls going after each other over a particular...uh...customer." Not wanting to cause Angela pain, he left out kidnapping and murder.

Eyes wide, Martha glanced at Angela, her mouth opening and closing. "Do wives enter saloons to locate their husbands?"

Shane swallowed a piece of steak with coffee, setting down the cup. "Sure. Not often. Maybe two or three times a year. Funniest sight you'll ever see."

"How would such a spectacle be funny?"

"Well, Miss van Plew, the wife is already angry at her husband for forcing her to extradite him from evil temptations. The resulting shouting and demands turns into a spectacle, until the man relents and leaves with his wife."

"Why would she object to playing cards and men drinking whiskey?" Martha asked.

Shane forced away his grin. "There's downstairs entertainment and upstairs entertainment at some saloons."

Frowning, Martha thought on this for a moment before her eyes grew wide. "You mean..."

Angela glared at Shane, knowing he'd steered the conversation in this direction. "Some men hire saloon women for extra services, which are performed in the privacy of their upstairs rooms."

"Prostitutes?"

Letting out an exasperated breath, Angela nodded. "Yes."

"Do you mean if I look inside a saloon, I might see one?"

"Perhaps."

"That would be so interesting. We must do it, Angela. When is the best time of day, Deputy Banderas?"

Rubbing his forehead, Shane stared down at his plate, wondering how their conversation had gotten so out of hand. Lifting his gaze to meet Martha's, he ignored Angela's warning glare.

"After supper is the best time."

"Excellent. We can peek inside one when we finish our meal."

"Martha, I don't think that's such a good idea."

"Why not, Angela? We won't be harming anyone, or breaking the law. Isn't that right, Deputy?"

Angela spoke up before Shane could answer, keeping her voice even. "It's a horrible idea. Those women aren't part of some spectacle. They work hard to make a living, and deserve a measure of privacy."

"I agree with much of what you're saying, except their privacy. After all, it's not as if we'd be breaking into the upstairs rooms to go through their belongings. We'd be taking a peek through the windows."

"I don't see the harm in Martha taking a look inside, Angie. I'm heading that way myself. You can walk along with me."

Shane showing up at their table had been unexpected. Angela hadn't been prepared to see him, or experience this other, kinder side of him. So similar to the man she'd fallen in love with all those years ago. The change from that morning was so drastic, Angela had a hard time understanding it.

"Why are you being so nice, Shane? This morning, you were prepared to put me on the stage, never set eyes on me again. Tonight, you're offering to escort us through town. I want to know what changed."

⁓⁓⁓

Arm in arm, Angela and Martha followed Shane along the boardwalk. Not yet seven, the Dixie was already full of men drinking and gambling, as was the Wild Rose across the street. Martha had wanted to stop, but Shane assured her neither offered the extra services provided by Finn's.

The short walk, and fresh air, gave Shane a few minutes to consider how to respond to Angela's demand. He didn't have an immediate answer. Martha had saved him from saying something he might later regret.

Ending the brief standoff, she'd stood. Announcing her intent to do what they'd discussed, Martha had grabbed her reticule before heading to the door. Angela had followed, giving him a look which told him she expected a response. Shane couldn't deny she deserved one.

Reaching Finn's, Shane motioned for them to stand by one of the windows. He stood behind them, pointing out the women known to provide the extras some men wanted.

"See the lady in the bright blue dress and red hair? That's Brenda. Finn introduces her as his daughter, but Gabe doesn't believe that's true. Regardless, she and her sister, Alana, deal with the women. Some just serve drinks. Others, such as the one wearing the emerald dress, serve and invite gentlemen upstairs."

Angela lifted a fine, arched brow. "Gentlemen?"

"A figure of speech, Angie. It may surprise you to learn most of the men treat the women well. The majority aren't married. They're ranch hands, drifters, single men who crave companionship for a brief spell. The woman in yellow has her hand on the gambler's shoulder. They'll be heading upstairs at some point."

"She's so young," Martha whispered.

"Most start out early. As young as fourteen. She's a little older, maybe seventeen."

Angela wondered how he knew this, deciding not to ask. It wasn't her business if Shane paid for a woman.

Martha glanced over her shoulder at Shane. "Have you ever used their services?"

"On occasion."

Angela felt her body jerk, hoping he didn't notice. "With any of the women we're watching?"

Leaning down, he whispered against her ear. "No, Angie. Not with any of the women in Splendor."

His warm breath fanned over her cheek and down her neck, bringing a rush of sensations she hadn't felt since before her father sent her to Boston. Shuddering, she had the craziest impulse to turn around, place her hands on his shoulders, and kiss him. Refusing to humiliate herself, she made the smart move and stepped away.

"I've seen enough. Are you ready to go home, Martha?"

"Yes. Thank you, Deputy, for escorting us."

"I'm heading home myself. I'll walk with you."

"Oh, that's not necessary. We'll be fine on our own," Angela objected, unable to bear another minute with him so close.

"I live a few houses from you. There's no reason to walk alone." Shane wouldn't admit he wasn't ready to part from her. He also refused to allow them to walk alone at night when Sutton and his men may be nearby.

"That's very thoughtful of you." Martha glanced around at the growing darkness and lack of gaslights. "I'd appreciate the escort. Angela?"

Licking her lips, she nodded. "All right."

Taking a route he didn't believe they knew about, he led them between the general store and McCall's restaurant. Passing Ruby's Grand Palace, he pointed out the meat market and bookstore.

"They opened over a year ago. The owner of the meat market purchases beef from the Pelletiers, and pork from a farmer south of town. Don't know where the chickens come from, but my guess is from the Murton ranch. Ty, Mark, and Gil provide turkeys and chickens to the Eagle's Nest, boardinghouse, and McCall's. They're real fine folks."

"What of the bookstore? Have you been inside?"

"Many times, Miss van Plew. If they don't have a book you want, they'll order it." Crossing a street, he pointed out the clinic. "Best doctors in Montana. Doc Worthington has been in Splendor since not long after it was founded. Doc McCord came along a few years later."

Martha studied the two story building, impressed with what she saw. "What about nurses?"

Shane thought of Carrie, and his plans to court her. "There are two. Georgina Wise and, uh...Carrie Galloway. They traveled together from New York."

Angela heard something in his voice, which made her heart squeeze. "Are you courting Miss Galloway?"

That was twice tonight she'd surprised him. "No."

The fact he intended to court her when Angela left Splendor didn't matter right now. The look of relief on her face caught him unaware. Did she care if he held an interest in another woman? Shaking off the question which would muddle his brain further, he stopped on their street, nodding to a house straight ahead.

"That's my house. At least for now."

"Are you leaving Splendor?" Martha asked the question Angela couldn't.

"I bought a cabin not far from town. Noah built it before marrying Abby. Someday, I hope to find the right woman, marry, and have children. The cabin would be perfect."

Angela couldn't look at him for the lump in her throat. After what she'd done, his words made it clear she wasn't the right woman.

A mischievous grin brightened Martha's face. "Do you have someone in mind?"

Stopping in front of their house, he looked at Angela. "Yes, I have someone in mind."

Instead of an image of Carrie, a memory of him and Angela popped into his head. They'd been walking near the river, their fingers entwined, stopping to kiss every few steps. Three or four times a week, they'd finish their chores and meet at the river. Being with Angela had become the highlight of each day.

Shaking off what could never be again, he focused on Angela's pale face.

Lifting her chin, Angela fought the pain at his last words. "Thank you for walking us home, and for the information. I hope the woman you have in mind knows what a wonderful man you are." The last came out as a choked whisper.

Racing up the stairs, she disappeared inside before the tears burning at the back of her eyes could fall.

Chapter Thirteen

"We went through each room, checked everywhere, and found nothing to confirm he's Shane Banderas, boss. But the description fits what you told us." Cal glanced at Jeb, who nodded in agreement.

"And he's a deputy," Jeb added.

Rand's inscrutable gaze studied the two young outlaws he'd sent ahead to confirm Shane still lived in Splendor. Of the lot, Cal Rivers and Jeb Franklin were the best. Careful, smart, and handy with a gun, they'd proven themselves more than once.

"Did you hear anyone call him by name?"

Cal shook his head. "We didn't want to get so close he might remember us. Do you want us to go back?"

"How do you know you got the right house?"

"We saw him go inside." Jeb shot a nervous look at Cal. They'd watched him shoot two of the gang for nothing more than having big mouths.

Already convinced the deputy his boys saw was the same man who'd plagued him from his arrest to the gallows, Rand considered sending them back for a different reason. Information was the key to bringing the man down. He wanted Banderas dead, and he would be the one pulling the trigger.

"It's late. Get some rest. I'll give you my decision in the morning."

Leaving them with the others, Rand pulled a cheroot from his pocket. Striking a match, he lit the end, inhaling as he walked away from their camp.

He did his best thinking late at night when the others were asleep. Taking a path toward a pond he'd spotted the night before, Rand thought of his best friend. The man Banderas had shot when the posse found them.

Hoot had been as close as a brother, his one true friend, a man Rand trusted. At ten, they'd fought over a piece of candy they'd stolen from a younger boy. They'd rolled around, punching, kicking, and biting each other until the sheriff and a deputy pulled them apart.

The deputy had taken him home to his drunken father, a man who'd enjoyed inflicting his misery on others. Most times on his only child. Rand never understood how he'd survived the vicious blows from his father that night. Five years later, with his father dead, Rand stole a horse and never looked back. Refusing to be left behind, Hoot rode with him.

Rand figured his hatred of all lawmen began the day he and his best friend fought over a piece of hard candy.

Lowering himself at the edge of the pond, he sat down, stretching out his legs. Even to his own eyes, they were scrawny. Chicken legs, Hoot had described them. His arms were no different.

At five-foot-seven, most men underestimated him. They noticed his stature, deciding Rand would be an easy target, when the opposite was true. He made a great deal of money from men who misjudged him.

Their secret weapon, Hoot had once called himself. A six-foot-four giant with thick arms and thicker thighs, he wouldn't show himself until Rand had drawn their quarry to him. One chop of Hoot's beefy hand had broken more necks than Rand could recall. Easy and quick, they'd taken what they wanted off the body and moved on.

Not that Rand couldn't fight. He was a scrapper, a fighter to his bones, using whatever means necessary to win.

It had been a sweet life, until Banderas had ended Hoot's. He'd never forget the sight of his friend bleeding out over the rocks of their makeshift hidey hole. Those days were long gone, but not the memories.

Tilting his head back, Rand stared at the ink black sky studded with more stars than he could ever count. Closing his eyes, he considered the boys' suggestion.

Cal and Jeb had done what he asked, returning to their camp on the agreed upon day and time. Rand had no doubt the deputy they followed was Shane Banderas. But there was more he needed before the gang rode into Splendor.

Decision made, Rand shoved to his feet. Returning to the camp, he shook his head in disgust. All the men were asleep except two, who stood as guards. Cal and Jeb.

Splendor

    Shane didn't walk straight home after escorting Angela and Martha to their door. It had been a pleasant stroll with him pointing out different businesses, and his experience with them.

    The sight of Angela fleeing inside had been unexpected. Shane scrubbed a hand down his face as he tried to remember if he'd said anything to upset her.

    After the debacle at Noah's saddlery, he'd decided to take a new approach. His mama often told him the best way to get what he wanted was with a spoonful of honey instead of vinegar. As a deputy, he'd decided to test his mama's words. Finding her right more often than not, Shane continued to use as much honey as he could stomach before resorting to tougher means.

    Spotting Angela and Martha entering the boardinghouse had been pure luck. The invitation to join them allowed Shane to try his new approach. They'd made it through dinner without a harsh word. But Angela had noticed the change and insisted he explain. He'd meant to give her some nonsense excuse before her quick departure.

    Walking past the lumber mill, he turned left on Grant Street. Chinatown to the locals, many purchased herbs, spices, silk fabric, and other items not offered elsewhere.

    Reaching the end of the street, he stopped, staring at Ruby's. Still early, he could hear the music coming from inside. From the laughter, hoots, and applause, Shane guessed Ruby's girls were entertaining on the large stage.

He considered buying a whiskey to see what new act Ruby had come up with for this week's entertainment. Opening the door, Shane got a whiff of the smoke mixed with sweat, and turned away. Realizing he wasn't in the mood for a crowd, he switched directions, heading toward the stream behind the boardinghouse.

Spotting the bench Noah had built and donated to the town, Shane settled himself on the seat. The surge of water had lessened since the spring thaw, leaving a calmer flow. As the town grew, more people started using the bench. Finding it empty had become a rare event.

Removing his hat, Shane removed the leather thong at the nape of his neck. Running fingers through the long strands, he returned to Angela's sudden exit into the house.

He'd noticed the change in her as they covered the last few yards to their house. What had they been talking about? The cabin. He'd mentioned leaving his house now that he had a cabin. Closing his eyes, his words came back to him.

"Someday, I hope to find the right woman, marry, and have children. The cabin would be perfect."

Opening his eyes, Shane blew out a curse. Angela's steps had faltered at his words, the expectant expression disappearing the same as an extinguished flame. Then Martha asked him if he had someone in mind. When he'd responded yes, Angela's face had paled. A moment later, she'd thanked him before dashing up the steps.

There was something he was missing. Pinching the bridge of his nose, her parting words, spoken in a choked whisper, came back to him.

"I hope the woman you have in mind knows what a wonderful man you are."

Heart hammering in his chest, Shane groaned. What he'd said about the cabin, marrying, and having children was true. Same with having someone in mind. Except, instead of an image of Carrie popping into his head, it had been Angela, smiling up at him as they held hands.

Could it be possible she'd traveled to Splendor because of him? This time, he didn't shove the idea aside. Why else would she have gone out of her way to a modest frontier town, instead of staying on the train to San Francisco?

It struck Shane how he'd never heard Angela's side of the story. He'd gone with the easiest explanation of her departure, instead of digging a little deeper when she'd come to Splendor with Carson. The fact they were engaged shouldn't have stopped him from seeking the truth.

"Ah, hell." He blew out a frustrated breath.

"Spoken like a man who's having trouble with a woman. May I?" Nick Barnett nodded to the empty space next to Shane. At his nod, Nick lowered himself onto the bench and pulled out a flask, handing it to Shane. "The universal cure for man's ineptitude when it comes to women."

Chuckling despite what weighed him down, Shane took a long swallow of whiskey.

"Feel better?" Nick accepted the flask from Shane, taking his own swig.

"Heck if I know, but I'm not going to refuse a drink from your private stash." It wasn't a secret Nick kept the best whiskey in his office, using it to fill the flask. The times were rare when he broke it out for others.

"I'm guessing Winslow's fiancée has you twisted into a knot."

"Former fiancée."

"I stand corrected." Slipping the flask back into the inside of his coat, Nick fell silent. Several minutes later, Shane broke the quiet.

"There's a good chance Angie came to Splendor because of me."

"I do believe you're right."

Glancing at Nick, Shane rubbed his jaw. "Why do you say that?"

"What woman in her right mind would exchange seats on the train to San Francisco for a stagecoach to Splendor? Not many, unless she had a good reason. Now, Miss Baldwin doesn't seem the type of woman to do anything without a purpose." Stretching out his legs, Nick crossed them at the ankles, resting his hands in his lap. "By the look of you when I walked up, I'd say her purpose and yours might not be the same."

"There's the problem. We haven't spoken about the real reason for her visit."

Nick gave a slow nod. "But you're thinking it's you." Standing, he held out his hand to Shane. "If you want some advice, don't let it fester too long before you talk. Women are tetchy about things like that."

Hours later, Shane lay on his bed, counting the planks in the ceiling. His first impulse when Nick walked up was to leave. He wouldn't have, but he longed for time alone to sort out his conflicting thoughts on Angela.

By the time Nick left, he'd been grateful for the older man's sage advice. Shane had to talk with Angela, understand what happened over six years ago, and learn her reason for coming to Splendor.

Seemed simple, yet his instincts warned him to tread with care. For all the pain she'd caused him, Shane believed Angela had suffered as well.

Both sought answers to a long list of questions. What plagued him, kept him awake late into the night, was unease over what the answers would bring. Would they solve anything, or cause more harm?

He knew with certainty, her leaving Splendor wasn't what he wanted. At least, not until they talked. Afterward, he'd sort out what to do next. Continue with his original plan to court Carrie, or take a chance he and Angela might still have a future.

Making up his mind, Shane closed his eyes, vowing the questions would begin tomorrow.

Chapter Fourteen

Loud pounding woke Shane at sunrise. Glancing at the mantel clock on his dresser, he groaned. Three hours of sleep wasn't long enough to clear the fuzziness in his head. Rolling out of bed as the pounding started again, he murmured a frustrated curse.

"I'm coming!"

Tripping over his pants, he snagged them, falling over in his attempt to slide his legs inside. Not bothering with a shirt or boots, he padded to the front door, rubbing his eyes. Opening the door, he jerked awake at the sight of Gabe.

"May I come in?"

Stepping aside, he rubbed his eyes again, scratching the back of his neck. "Sit down. Let me make coffee."

"No time right now. I have to ride to the Pelletier ranch, so I'll make this quick. I need you to ride to the MacLaren spread east of town. Thane rode in late yesterday to report five of their steers are missing. They searched all day without luck. When they didn't find them, Bram had Thane ride to town." Gabe reached into a pocket, pulling out a folded piece of paper. "These are my notes. I want you to talk with Bram and the Latham brothers about what they saw during the search."

"I'll have the information for you when you return from Redemption's Edge."

"There's more. Don't return to town. You're needed in Big Pine. I received a letter from Sheriff Sterling. There's a prisoner who was convicted of stealing items from various stores. You're to escort him to Splendor. As you know, my brother, Chan, is tasked with this, but he's on his way to the prison at Deer Lodge."

Shane thought of his decision to speak with Angela today, disappointed it would be delayed. Their conversation would have to wait until he returned.

"Do you want me to take an extra horse?"

Gabe shook his head. "Sterling will have a mount ready for the prisoner. I'd send another deputy with you, but I'll need everyone if Sutton appears."

Shane's lips pressed into a hard line. "You're sending me so I'm gone if Sutton arrives."

"Yes and no. Most of the others are married, some with children. This could be a three day round trip. We've been watching for several days and nights without seeing a hint of Sutton's gang. I don't know what that means, but we can't put off our regular work on the chance they'll show up. How soon can you leave?"

"Give me thirty minutes to pack my saddlebags and eat breakfast. Is that soon enough?"

"It is. And I appreciate it, Shane. I'd best get going myself."

"If you have another minute, someone broke into my house. With all that's going on, I forgot to report it earlier."

Gabe's brows furrowed as he released a sigh. Lowering himself into a chair, he motioned for Shane to do the same. "Sit down and tell me everything."

Explaining what he found, he ended by saying there was nothing missing. "I don't know why someone would take the risk if they didn't plan to steal anything, but I do have my suspicions."

"To learn more about you. It's a common practice in larger towns. Confirm who lives in the house, how vulnerable the occupants are, and decide whether to proceed or forget whatever they had planned. In your case, I believe someone wants to know who's living in the house."

Even though his thoughts had been heading in that direction, it took a moment before the pieces began to fit together. "Sutton sent men to town to confirm I'm here and where I live."

"Which means they were right under our noses and we didn't know it."

Jumping up, Shane paced several steps away before whirling to face Gabe. "Angela Baldwin and Martha van Plew moved into the house next door to Dutch. Whoever's been spying on me may have seen me with them. I walked them home after supper last night."

"I'll make sure Dutch keeps watch on them while you're gone." Gabe stood, moving to the door. "Anything else?"

"Maybe have Dutch tell them where I am. I, well..."

"You don't have to say more. I'll pass the word to Dutch."

Closing the door behind Gabe, Shane didn't move for several moments as he digested what the sheriff said. It all made a horrible kind of sense.

He thought of Angela and Martha, and the possible danger. An intense ache grew in his chest. The type of ache he experienced after he'd been told she died. Then again when she'd arrived in Splendor, very much alive. Rubbing the spot with the palm of his hand, he tried not to think about what his reaction meant.

Stalking to the bedroom, he stuffed the saddlebags with clothes, an extra revolver, and ammunition. Moving to the kitchen, he wrapped hard tack and jerky in a cloth, adding them to the bags. It took little time to finish dressing before grabbing his rifle for the walk to Noah's.

The sky was still dark as he passed Angela's house, wishing he could see her before leaving. He'd trust Gabe's word, knowing Dutch would get the message to her.

Noah hadn't arrived by the time he tacked up his stallion. Leaving a brief note tacked to the livery door, he rode out the gate, closing it behind him.

⁓⁓⁓

Cal and Jeb left their horses at the same place Sutton had chosen the last time. He'd insisted they ride into town on the stage when first arriving, insisting it would draw less attention. From their location, the walk to town would be short.

As they hoped, no one noticed them step onto the boardwalk across from the St. James. Hungry from their early ride out of camp, they sat down at a table in McCall's, seeing Betts come toward them with two cups filled with coffee.

"Haven't seen you boys in a couple days. You find another place to eat?" Betts accompanied her slight reprimand with a huge smile.

"You know we have to spread our money around, ma'am." Cal stirred sugar into the coffee, his eyes sparkling with mirth. "But you're still our favorite."

Chuckling, she looked between the two. "You boys are too charming for your young age. What can I get you?"

Ordering, they hunkered over their cups, lowering their voices.

"How are we going to get a true count of the number of deputies, Jeb? From what we saw last, there are more than Sutton thinks."

Cal glanced out the front window, noticing one of the deputies across the street. "They seem to stop at the Dixie or Wild Rose in the afternoons."

"They always stand at the bar," Jeb added. "You're thinking each of us goes to one of them, starts a conversation, and asks them."

"Might be good to ask if they need more deputies."

They leaned back in their chairs as Betts set the plates in front of them. "I'll bring more coffee. Let me know if you want anything else."

Cal picked up his fork, licking his lips. "Thank you, ma'am. This all looks real good."

"Smells good, too." Jeb placed a forkful of eggs in his mouth, and grinned.

"I'll leave you boys alone."

Tucking into their meal, neither spoke until they'd finished every bite. Pushing the plates aside, they again leaned toward each other.

"What about the other?" Jeb's face twisted, indicating what he thought of Rand's order.

"How would I know?" Cal drummed his fingers on the wood table. "Doesn't sit right with me."

"Threatening women isn't why I joined the gang. Thought we were going to rob banks, stages, and trains. This?" Jeb shook his head before taking another sip of coffee.

"Gotta tell you, I feel the same. We could always get our horses and ride off."

Staring out the window, Jeb seemed to be considering their choices. "We don't have much money. Rand isn't the kind of man to forget being betrayed."

"You think he'll come after us?"

"After seeing him gun down two of the boys, I'm inclined to think he would. The man's a powder keg, always ready to blow."

"I know you're finished eating, but thought I'd bring out a few slices of my sweet bread." Setting the plate down, she filled their cups again. "You won't be charged for the bread."

Jeb eyed the slices, his stomach already reacting to the enticing aroma. "Thank you, ma'am. That's real nice of you."

Betts didn't get far away from their table before they grabbed slices, taking large bites.

"Haven't had sweet bread since leaving home. Ma used to make at least one loaf every week." Swallowing some coffee, Jeb finished, picking up another slice. "This is almost as good."

"I remember your ma's sweet bread. Also her pies and cakes. She was a darn fine cook." Grabbing the last slice, it took just two bites for Cal to finish. "Damn cancer took her too soon."

Jeb swallowed, thinking of his mother. Slender as a willow, with large gray eyes, and brown hair always worn in a bun, she'd had a hard life after her husband left her. Jeb and his sister stayed behind, knowing their mother would need help to keep up the farm. Cal, whose uncle took him in when his parents left to find gold in California, often helped with the chores, taking supper with them most nights. Then the cancer came.

At eighteen, his sister was of an age to marry, which is what she did a couple months after the funeral. Having no interest in farming, Jeb sold it to a widowed rancher who intended to breed horses. He'd offered half to his sister, who refused, saying her husband did well as the local banker and owner of several buildings in town.

Talking Cal into leaving with him, the two rode west, having no particular plans other than getting away from the hard work of farming. Odd jobs had sustained them, along with the occasional draw from the sale of the farm. Riding through Texas, they'd landed in The Flat.

"We've gotta decide what to do next, Jeb. Do as Rand ordered or take off."

Dragging fingers across his brow, Jeb pulled money from his pocket, and stood. "Let's get out of here."

Turning left out of McCall's, they covered the short distance to the newest business in Splendor. Three miners, too old to continue the hard labor required, had opened a second boardinghouse across from the church.

Cheaper than the one Suzanne Barnett owned, with smaller rooms, the food wasn't as good, but there was lots of it. Perfect for the two of them.

"Gents. Thought you two had left town." The oldest of the three miners stood at the counter, a match bobbing up and down between his teeth. "One room or two?"

"Same as last time," Cal answered. "One room with two beds."

"How many nights you gonna be here?"

"Two, maybe more. I'll pay you for those, then more if we stay longer." Reaching into his pocket, Cal set a couple coins on the counter.

"Upstairs. Third room on the right." The grizzled miner handed Cal a key. "You know when we serve meals. Don't expect anything if you're late."

"Yeah, we know. Thanks." Cal bounded up the stairs to their room, Jeb right behind him.

Each plopped down on a bed, Cal falling back on the mattress, while Jeb scooted to the headboard. Rather, a three by three piece of wood nailed to the wall.

Several minutes passed before Jeb spoke. "I'm not kidnapping any women. Fact is, I'm not taking anyone so Rand can claim his vengeance."

Cal didn't respond right away, thinking about their boss's order. "We'll learn what we can from the deputies, get it back to Rand, telling him we need more time to dig up information on the women."

"Then what?"

Grinning, Cal turned toward Jeb. "We ride right past Splendor and just keep going."

Chapter Fifteen

"Where do you get these glorious tomatoes?" Angela held one up to her nose, grinning at the clerk in the meat market. An older man, she suspected he was the owner.

"A farm south of here. Tomatoes, green beans, onions, carrots, turnips, potatoes, and corn." He pointed to each as he spoke. "All come from there, plus pork. The beef is from the Pelletier ranch, the chickens from the Murton brothers."

Angela recalled Shane saying the same. "Do they bring you the meat and vegetables every day?"

"Three days a week. Monday, Wednesday, and Friday. It's not often I have anything left over by the time I close on Saturday."

She was impressed. There were stores in Boston who didn't get fresh goods that often. "I'll take two tomatoes, four carrots, a half pound of beans, an onion, and a pound of stew meat."

As she spoke, he set the items on the counter. "I don't usually cut the meat, but will be happy to for you, miss. It'll be a couple minutes."

"No hurry. I'll look at what else you have while I wait."

Joining Martha in a corner of the store, she found her looking at loaves of fresh bread. Holding one up, she breathed in the yeasty aroma. "This would be wonderful with our stew."

Taking it from her, Angela took it to the clerk. "Do you make the bread here?"

A broad, proud smile brightened his face. "My wife makes it every morning. Gets up at four o'clock. We sell several loaves a day here, the rest goes to McCall's and Suzanne Barnett's boardinghouse restaurant, plus a few loaves to the new boardinghouse at the end of the street."

Impressed, Angela placed the bread next to her other purchases. "One loaf, please."

"Certainly, Miss..."

"Baldwin. My friend is Miss van Plew. We're staying in the house next to Deputy McFarlin."

"Oh, yes. Dutch's place. He's one of our best customers. I'm Mr. Caulfield. It's nice to meet you, ladies. Would you like my boy to deliver your purchases?"

"That would be wonderful. We have a few more errands to run first. Could you send him after two this afternoon?"

"Sure can. Hope to see you again real soon."

"I'm certain you will, Mr. Caulfield. Shall we continue, Martha?"

The bookstore was next. Selecting several books from a variety larger than either expected, they moved on to the general store. Rounding a corner, they just missed running into two young men.

"Sorry, ladies." Cal touched the brim of his hat.

"We didn't see you coming." Jeb touched his as well before moving aside.

Studying them a moment, Angela realized where she'd seen them. "I believe we've seen you in the boardinghouse restaurant, gentlemen. You had just arrived on the stage."

"Oh, yes. I remember them now," Martha added. "It was several days ago, so I doubt you'd remember."

"Can't forget two beautiful ladies such as yourselves." The truth was, Cal did remember them. "Perhaps one day, you'll allow us to buy you lunch or supper."

Blushing, Martha glanced at Angela.

"Perhaps, gentlemen. I'm Miss Baldwin, and this is Miss van Plew. We're visiting from Boston. And you are?"

Realizing they may have found the women Rand wanted them to meet, Cal removed his hat. "Cal Rivers, and this is Jeb Franklin. Pleased to meet you, ladies. We're also new in town."

"Well, we have more errands before returning home." Slipping her arm through Angela's, Martha began moving away.

"You'll hear from us soon, ladies," Cal called as the women walked down the boardwalk. When they were out of earshot, he turned toward Jeb. "That's them."

Nodding, Jeb fingered the butt of his gun, even more certain he wouldn't be carrying out all of Rand's orders. "Thought so."

Shifting his gaze across the street to the Dixie, Cal spotted one of the deputies enter the saloon. "I'm going to see if the deputy will talk. Why don't you head to the Wild Rose? We'll meet at our room before supper."

MacLaren Ranch

"You didn't see any tracks indicating the steers were stolen, Bram?" Shane leaned forward in his saddle, watching the small herd from their spot on a low hill.

"Nothing. Vince Latham rode out at dawn to do the count and relieve one of the new ranch hands. Since the herd isn't large, it doesn't take much time to check the number. Five were missing. Vince sent the ranch hand back to notify me and Thane. Kev Latham rode back with us and searched for close to five hours. No tracks. Nothing to indicate what happened to them. All we know is they're gone."

Thane took a step closer to the men. "We thought it best to report the missing cattle so there's a record. Maybe other ranchers have lost cattle, too."

"Haven't heard of any, but you did the right thing." Rubbing his chin, Shane looked around. "Could they have been taken by the Blackfoot renegades who've been causing trouble around here?"

Removing his hat, Bram raked fingers through his hair. "Could've been anyone. The Blackfoot are one possibility. Wish we had more for you."

"You reported the cattle missing, which will help if any other ranchers find their count short."

"Regardless, we appreciate you riding out. You want to ride back to the house? Selina made pie last night and always has coffee ready."

"Thanks for the offer, Bram, but I have to ride to Big Pine. There's a prisoner I need to escort to Splendor."

"Next time. You're always welcome. We'd better head back, Thane."

Shane stayed a little longer, watching the MacLarens ride off. He wanted to return to Splendor, tell Gabe what he'd learned, and talk to Angela.

His orders were specific. Ride on to Big Pine. And that's what he'd do. If all went well, Shane would collect the prisoner, return to Splendor by tomorrow night, and go straight to Angela's.

~~~

Shane didn't expect to cross paths with the afternoon stage going between Big Pine and Splendor. By his reckoning, it was at least three hours late. Waving an arm, he reined to a stop as the stage did the same. Recognizing him, the driver leaned down from his perch on the bench.

"Guess you already learned about the trouble in Big Pine, Deputy."

Shane edged his horse closer to the side of the stage. "Don't know what you're talking about."

"The bank robbery. Five outlaws took over the Territorial Bank of Montana at the east end of town. Got away with over twenty thousand dollars."

"Anyone recognize them?" Although Shane had already guessed who they were.

"Their faces were covered. No one knew what was happening until a few minutes before the outlaws rode out. We stayed long enough for the sheriff to speak with my passengers, and to be sure the gang hadn't changed direction and headed west."

"Was anyone hurt?"

"Not a single injury. The older couple inside the coach got a decent view of the outlaws going inside and leaving. They'd never be able to identify them, though."

Leaning down, Shane got a look at the passengers. One older couple, a younger couple, and a lone man. "Guess you folks had some excitement today." If he remembered right, the stage office wasn't far from the bank.

The older woman spoke up first. "Yes, we did, young man. More than I want to see again. Those poor people in the bank."

The older man, Shane guessed to be her husband, placed a hand over hers. "Now, dear. No one was hurt. They'll be fine."

"Any of you staying in Splendor for long?"

"The four of us are staying overnight, Deputy," the younger woman answered. "Tomorrow, we'll catch the next stage toward the west. I believe this gentleman is staying." She nodded to the middle-aged man next to her.

Wearing what might've been a black suit and bowler hat when their journey started, the somewhat rotund man's clothes were now covered in a thick layer of trail dust.

"Do you have kin in Splendor?"

Looking up from where he'd been staring at his clenched hands, the man shook his head. "No. I have business to attend to, then I'll be going back east. That is, if the woman I seek hasn't gone on to San Francisco."

Shane's chest tightened. He'd heard the flat accent before. "Where'd you travel from?"

"Boston."

The answer he didn't want to hear, but expected. "Perhaps I've met the woman you're talking about."

"I'm certain you wouldn't know her."

Shane shrugged. "As a deputy, I know a great number of people in town."

Huffing out a resigned sigh, the man lifted his chin. "Miss Angela Baldwin. Prior to his death, she was engaged to Carson Winslow. Of the Boston Winslows." A self-satisfied smirk shifted the man's expression from haughty to superior.

"Yes, I know her." Straightening in his saddle, Shane looked at the driver, missing the man's stunned expression. "I'd better get to Big Pine. Have a safe journey."

Whirling his horse around, he kicked the horse into a canter. Shane had no idea what the man's business was with Angela, but it had to be important for him to make the trip thousands of miles to talk with her.

His trip had taken on a new urgency. If he could talk Sheriff Sterling into it, Shane would collect the prisoner and ride back to Splendor tonight. Now that she'd returned to Splendor, Shane didn't plan to let Angela leave before hearing her side of the story.

***

"Miss Baldwin. Miss van Plew." Passing them on the boardwalk, arms laden with purchases, Deputy Jonas Taylor tipped his hat to them. "Where are you headed?"

"We're renting the house next to Deputy McFarlin." Martha juggled a large package, almost dropping it before Jonas scooped it away. Turning, he took another from Angela. "Can't have you dropping all your new purchases."

Passing Ruby's, another deputy joined them. "Who do we have here?"

A scowl passed over Jonas's face before he could conceal it. "Miss van Plew and Miss Angela Baldwin. They're from Boston. Ladies, this is Deputy Tucker Nolan."

Tucker plucked the remaining packages from each of them. "Where are we headed, Jonas?"

"They've rented the house next to Dutch's."

Tucker grinned at the women. "You're real close to us. We're in the house next to the clinic."

"Is it the two of you?" Martha asked.

Jonas glanced over at her. "Another deputy, Morgan Wheeler, lives with us. We've all been friends for years."

Shooting a quick look at Angela, Martha returned her attention to Jonas. "Perhaps we could have the three of you over for supper sometime. When you aren't working, of course."

"We'd never turn down home-cooked food, ma'am." Jonas shot another fleeting glance at Martha. She was about the prettiest thing he'd ever seen.

"Wonderful. Please let us know when all of you are available." Martha hid a private smile, quite pleased with herself for being so bold.

Reaching their house, Angela opened the front door, motioning them inside. "Thank you for assisting us, gentlemen."

Martha glanced between the two quite handsome men as they laid the packages on the kitchen table. "Yes. Your help was quite unexpected."

Tipping his hat, Jonas winked at her. "Our pleasure, ma'am."

Tucker nodded. "If you're sure about the invitation, we'll be sure and let you know when all three of us are available."

"Please do. We'll be happy to have you join us." Closing the door, Martha whirled around, leaning her back against it. "Weren't they wonderful, Angela?"

A knock on the door had her hurrying to open it. Hoping it was Jonas and Tucker, her features sagged a little to find a young lad carrying two burlap bags.

"I have your purchases from my family's meat market, ma'am. Can I bring them inside?"

Drawing the door wide, Martha pointed toward the kitchen. "On the table would be fine." Opening her reticule, Angela pulled out two coins, handing them to him.

Eyes wide, he took them. "Two coins? Thank you, ma'am." Without another word, he dashed out the door and up the street.

Watching the boy skip away, Angela closed the door, her mind going to what they'd cook when the three deputies came for supper. The thought conjured up another image of another deputy. A good man. Handsome, proud, and dedicated to his job.

A man she was desperate to have back in her life.

Chapter Sixteen

Big Pine

"Do you think it was Rand Sutton and his men?" Shane sat in Sheriff Parker Sterling's office, legs stretched out to relieve the tight muscles after the long ride.

Scratching his chin, Sterling's mouth twisted. "Might've been. No one got a good look at the outlaws. There were five. They were smart. The bank manager said they communicated with hand signals instead of talking. I've sent telegrams to warn the other towns."

Shane had never heard of Sutton using hand signals, or using so few men. The outlaw enjoyed the notoriety, the attention received, knowing he'd led the gang who cleaned out banks, stages, and trains.

The fact a shot hadn't been fired also pointed away from Sutton. He'd ended at least one life with every robbery. Sometimes as many as half a dozen.

"What other gangs have been spotted in the territory?"

Placing his boots on the scarred desk and crossing them at the ankles, Sterling leaned back in his chair. "None. Sutton and his gang are all we've heard about."

"Nothing about the bank robbery fits how Sutton works. Still..."

Sterling narrowed his gaze on Shane. "Spit it out, son."

"Something's bothering me. I'm not ready to dismiss Sutton as a possibility."

Slamming his boots back on the floor, Sterling leaned forward, placing his arms on the desk. "I'm listening."

Shane rubbed a finger across his lower lip, recalling the vicious way Sutton and his gang committed their crimes. Today's robbery didn't fit, yet he couldn't dismiss the idea Sutton was behind it.

"A lot of his men were killed or scattered when the posse surrounded and arrested Rand. The ones we didn't capture are the men who helped him escape. The best count was four men in Cheyenne. Could've been more. His gang usually consists of more. It's the reason he always hits targets with big payloads."

"A lot of mouths to feed," Sterling commented.

"Did anyone provide a description of the outlaws?"

"The bank manager said they were all tall and lean. Others in the bank swore the men were shorter and muscled. An older man on the stage told me one was short and wiry, the others taller. Two of them more stout, the other two slim. He said all wore black, something no one else mentioned. I tend to believe his descriptions are the most accurate."

"Why's that?" At last, Shane thought he was getting something useful.

"Those in the bank were scared, some still shaking when I spoke with them. The man inside the stage wasn't in danger. Never seen a bystander as relaxed as that gent."

Shane thought of the older man he'd met on the stage, along with the middle-aged man from Boston. Getting the prisoner back to Splendor changed from important to urgent.

"Do you have a problem with me leaving tonight with the prisoner?"

"Doesn't matter to me. Just watch for the renegade Crow bandits. They keep watch at night, attacking small groups of riders. Two would make an easy target."

It had taken both Sterling and Shane to rouse the convicted thief from a sound sleep. At five-foot-six, the prisoner was pudgy, with a bushy head of dark hair, and patches of what Shane assumed was a developing beard on an otherwise smooth face. With a shock, he realized the prisoner couldn't be more than sixteen.

"Harley, you gotta get up for the trip to Splendor." A sleepy grunt was all the response Sterling received. "You take one arm, Shane, and I'll take the other."

Groaning with the effort, they pulled Harley to his feet, bracing him with their hands. Opening his eyes to slits, the young man shook his head before his blurry gaze shifted between the two men.

"Hey, Sheriff Sterling. What are you doing here?"

Parker's voice softened at Harley's confused expression. "Do you remember where you are, Harley?"

Face paling, he stared down at his stocking feet. "I think so. Do I have to leave Big Pine, Sheriff?"

Shane's confused gaze latched on Sterling. This wasn't at all what he'd expected. Most prisoners were foulmouthed and combative when faced with years in prison. Harley didn't appear to understand the future ahead of him.

"Sheriff, we should talk."

Giving a slow nod, they helped Harley to sit down on the wood bed topped with a thin mattress. Leaving the cell, Parker led the way to the front.

"Guess you're wondering what's going on."

Crossing his arms, Shane's impassive expression belied his frustration. "What are you not telling me?"

Scrubbing a hand down his face, Sterling lowered himself into his chair. "Gabe didn't explain?"

"Not a word."

Blowing out a sigh, Sterling pointed to a chair. "Sit down. I'll get a crick in my neck looking up at you."

Keeping his gaze on the sheriff, Shane sat down. "Tell me what I don't know."

"That boy in there has had a bad life. Real bad. His mother tried to leave with Harley about a year after his birth, taking his older brother with them. Her husband, Dale Sloan, found out, beat her until she almost died." Sterling glanced away, in a useless attempt to hide his anger. "He's mean, and can't get through a day without a bottle of whiskey. Two some days."

"Did you arrest him for assault?"

"The problem was the boys. Their mother was in the hospital, leaving their father to take care of them. Harriet begged me not to arrest him. As it turned out, he took off with what little money they had. The church women took care of the boys until Harriet was well enough to take over."

"With no money?"

Sterling's face reddened. "Some of the townsfolk helped out. Harriet took in laundry, did some sewing, cooked for an older couple." A wistful expression crossed the sheriff's face. "I'd never seen her so happy. Then her worthless husband came back. Harriet refused to let him into the house. What'd he do? Using a bottle of whiskey, Dale tried to set fire to the house."

Leaning forward, Shane's jaw tightened. "With his family inside?"

Mouth twisting into a sneer, Sterling nodded. "A deputy saw him. He spent a few days in jail before the trial. Judge sentenced him to a year at Deer Lodge. That was years ago. Harriet hasn't heard from him since."

"What does all this have to do with Harley?"

Sterling shot a look toward the cells. "He's sixteen. Nice kid, but isn't all there, if you know what I mean. Harriet has tried, but he's never understood the difference between buying and stealing. Wouldn't do any good to send him to Deer Lodge. He'd be dead within a month."

Leaning back in his chair, Shane crossed his arms. "Then why am I here?"

"Harley doesn't know the town thinks he's going to prison because of stealing. Let me tell you, the townsfolk aren't happy about. Still, that's the story we put together so if it gets to his father, he'll think his son is at Deer Lodge. Instead, Judge Collins requested Gabe's help in finding a home for him in Splendor. The Pelletiers have agreed to hire him."

"Why not send him there on the stage? It doesn't make sense to send a deputy to escort him to Splendor."

"His father."

Brows scrunching together, Shane stole a look over his shoulder at Harley's loud snore. "I thought no one had seen him since serving his time at Deer Lodge."

"A week ago, a friend of Harriet's told me she saw him leaving a saloon. He'd grown a beard, and his hair had a lot more gray, but she's certain it was him. The older son left to work on a local ranch. Harriet is afraid for Harley's safety. The judge, Gabe, and I came up with this solution. If we didn't, Harley would never leave his mother. If he believes it's his mother's wish he go, he won't fight us."

"You mean fight *me*," Shane mumbled.

"He won't cause problems for you. Harley's good people. You give him a task, he'll do it." Standing, Sterling walked toward the cells, stopping to turn back. "Take him to Gabe. He'll get him to the Pelletiers. His father will never find Harley there."

"You believe the man is that much of a danger to his own son?"

"That's exactly what I believe."

Shane didn't bother waking Gabe after arriving in Splendor a little before midnight. There had been no surprises on the ride from Big Pine. His biggest challenge was keeping Harley from falling asleep and tumbling to the ground.

The two lanterns inside the jail shone as a beacon when he reined to a stop. He didn't know which deputies were on duty. It didn't matter. All he had to do was secure Harley in a cell for the night. Shane would collapse on a bunk close by, not wanting the young man to wake without having someone he recognized nearby.

Helping Harley to the ground, he guided him into the jail, relieved to see Dutch McFarlin at the desk. Without explanation, Shane placed an exhausted Harley on a metal bed topped with an overstuffed mattress, settling a blanket over him.

"That pup an outlaw?" Dutch leaned a shoulder against the wall separating the front of the jail to the cells in back. "Looks to be about twelve."

"He's sixteen, and Harley's no outlaw. If you pour me a cup of coffee, I'll explain."

"Just so happens there's a fresh pot on the stove." Dutch poured two cups, setting both on the desk before easing into a chair.

Across from him, Shane lifted his cup, taking a sip. An appreciative smile curved his lips. "Best coffee this side of the Mississippi."

Thirty minutes later, Harley's story had been told. An incredulous expression transformed Dutch's passive face. "You mean his father plans to kill him?"

Stalking across the room to grab the coffeepot, Shane filled each cup again.

"That's what Judge Collins and Sheriff Sterling believe, and they convinced Gabe to help out. Doesn't matter, the Pelletiers have agreed to hire him. Can't believe a no-good drunk would be able to track his son down to Redemption's Edge. I think Harley's a bargaining chip between his ma and pa."

Scratching his chin, Dutch nodded. "Use the son as leverage to get his wife back."

"That's what Sterling believes, and it makes sense to me. From what he said, Harriet will never take the man back. She'd die before inviting him into her home." Shane jumped, drawing his gun when the jail door slammed open. His jaw dropped at the sight of the three new deputies laughing as they stumbled into the jail. "What in the world?"

"Hey, Shane. You're back early." Jonas steadied himself with a hand on the edge of the desk.

Tucker grabbed a chair, belching as he fell onto the seat. Morgan entered last, kicking Jonas's feet out from under him. Sprawling on the floor, Jonas glared up at his friend.

"Hey. What was that for?"

Crossing his arms, Morgan shook his head. "You're supposed to be sleeping at home. Not finishing off a bottle of whiskey outside Finn's." Lifting his head, Morgan's mouth twisted in disgust. "These two miscreants spent an hour at the Wild Rose, then moved to the Dixie before ending up at Finn's. The idiots are supposed to meet Gabe here at seven this morning. He wants them to ride to a ranch south of town about missing cattle."

Holstering his gun, Shane returned to his chair, recalling his meeting with the MacLarens. He had questions, but would save them for Gabe.

Taking another sip of coffee, Shane leaned back in his chair. "Why were they drinking?"

"Celebrating."

Dutch settled his muscled arms on the desk. "What do they have to celebrate?"

"Darn fools believe those two city women are going to take a liking to them."

Shane's stomach lurched, back stiffening. "What city women?"

"Miss Baldwin and Miss van Plew. They invited us to supper, and these idiots think it's more than just a meal. Anyone can see they're ladies, not a couple of loose women." Shaking his head, Morgan grabbed a chair, turning it around to rest his arms on the back. "It was nice of them to offer a home-cooked meal, but anyone can tell we're way below what they deserve."

Shane thought he heard a wistful tone to Morgan's comment, dismissing it to attack the issue of supper with Angela and Martha.

"You can tell them Miss Baldwin isn't available."

Dutch's eyes widened, as did Morgan's, wondering if they heard right.

Shoving back his chair, Shane stood. "Don't wait for an explanation. There isn't going to be one. Dutch, I'd appreciate you keeping watch on Harley."

Before either of the deputies could utter a word, Shane stalked out of the jail, his head pounding, jaw clenching at the latest news.

Chapter Seventeen

Tugging the ties of the apron, Angela secured it around her waist. A partial slab of bacon and four eggs lay next to the stove, two thick slices of Mrs. Caulfield's bread nearby. More than enough food for her and Martha.

"Where should I put this?"

Glancing to the back door, she smiled at the sight of Martha, arms laden with wood. Stepping aside, Angela nodded at the large, metal box by the stove. "Right here. I've already added what's needed for breakfast."

"I almost forgot. What did the man who arrived on the stage want?" Dropping the wood in the container, Martha brushed splinters and dirt from her brown dress.

"He had documents I needed to sign before all the assets transfer to my bank account. I met him at the bank so Mr. Clausen could attest to the signatures. Afterward, he boarded the next stage east."

Shrugging, Martha glanced over Angela's shoulder. "It's a great deal of work to fix breakfast, isn't it?"

Placing slices of bacon in the iron skillet, Angela used a wood spatula to move them around. "All meals take work. Put on the other apron so you can help."

"Me? I don't know anything about cooking bacon and eggs."

"You didn't know anything about making stew either, but you learned." Angela continued to move the slices, cooking them in the increasing amount of fat.

Grabbing the apron, Martha tied it around her waist. "Nothing smells as good as fried bacon."

Handing her the spatula, Angela stepped aside. "Watch for grease splatters so you don't burn yourself. When the bacon is crispy, but not black, move the slices to this plate."

Martha gazed down at the bacon, lips curled in as she concentrated on the task. She'd done the same with the stew, determined not to ruin supper.

A hard knock on the door surprised them both. Leaving her apron on, Angela took a quick look into the frying pan. "They're almost done, Martha."

When the knocking began again, she hurried to the door, pulling it open and stilled.

His eyes lit at the shock on her face. "Good morning, Angela."

"Shane. Um...what are you doing here?"

Inhaling, he pinned her with a wide grin. "For breakfast. I believe you invited the deputies over for a meal. I'm the deputy who's taking you up on it."

"The invitation was for Jonas, Morgan, and Tucker," she sputtered, licking her dry lips.

Rocking back on his heels, his smile never dimmed. "I forgot to mention, they're too busy. You know, being new to Splendor and all. Seems I'm the only deputy available."

From behind Angela, Martha turned from the stove. "Good morning, Deputy Banderas."

"Ma'am."

"Are you going to stand there, Angela, or let the starving man in?"

"She's right. My apologies. By all means, please join us for breakfast." Returning to the kitchen, Angela sliced several more pieces of bacon, adding them to the pan. "We're having eggs, bacon, and Mrs. Caulfield's bread."

"And jam from the general store," Martha added. "We were told it is quite good."

Setting his hat on the sofa, he took a step toward them. "It is. The same with anything Mrs. Caulfield bakes. Did you get the bacon from her husband?"

"Yes, and the beef we used for a stew. Their market is quite impressive." Setting four more eggs on the counter, Angela counted out three plates and utensils, hoping Shane didn't notice how her hands shook.

Being this close to him, remembering how they'd once been inseparable, hurt more than she'd ever admit. If Angela could go back in time, she would've tried harder to contact him, explain her circumstances. Instead, she'd been afraid of the consequences. The senior Winslow had been a stern taskmaster, doling out punishment more often than praise.

"I'll set the table while you help Martha." Shane took the plates and utensils from her, nodding toward the woman at the stove.

The change in mood from a hostile ex-suitor trying to run her out of town, to a charming gentleman, still had her head spinning. The Shane she remembered made a decision and stuck with it.

People changed, along with their feelings for others. It was hard to accept he wasn't the same person she'd known growing up, no longer holding the love for her he once had.

Wasn't that the reason Angela had traveled to Splendor? To learn if he still held feelings for her? Her heart squeezed, believing she had the answer.

"Would you mind helping me with the eggs, Angela?"

Lost in her own thoughts, she turned toward the stove, seeing Martha and Shane watching her. "Of course I'll help."

Ignoring their curious expressions, Angela picked up an egg, cracked the shell, and emptied it into a bowl. She did the same two more times before shoving the bowl toward Martha.

"Your turn."

Shooting a nervous glance at Angela and Shane, she cracked the shell against the side of the bowl, grinning when the contents slid on top of the other eggs. "I did it."

"You did. Just a few to go before we finish." Angela shot a glance at Shane, stomach churning at the genuine smile aimed at her.

Half an hour later, the meal finished and dishes washed, Angela stood next to the sofa. Martha and Shane stood close to each other, laughing at something one of them said. The sight shouldn't have bothered her, yet it did.

"Are you working today?" The question broke from her before Angela realized she'd spoken.

Grabbing his hat on the way to her, he fingered the brim. "Do you have time for a walk?"

She hadn't been prepared for the question. "What?"

"A walk, Angie. Around town. With me."

Stiffening, she crossed her arms, glaring at him. "I know what a walk is. What I don't understand is why you want to take one with me. A few days ago, you couldn't stand being near me. You do realize the walk you describe would mean people in town would see us, perhaps assume there is more than dislike for each other."

Clearing her throat, Martha motioned toward her bedroom. "I'll see both of you later."

Glad for her exit, Shane leaned to within inches of Angela's face, his voice low and soft. "I don't dislike you, Angie. Not even a little."

Opening her mouth, she snapped it shut, having no response. A minute passed before she found her voice. "A walk?"

"Yes."

It was what she'd wanted since returning to Splendor. Time alone with Shane, to talk, explain her side of what happened. Why the hesitancy?

"All right. I should let Martha know."

Chuckling, Shane noted the closed door to her bedroom. "I believe she already knows."

Opening the front door, he followed her outside. Taking her hand, he slid her arm through his, as if it hadn't been over six years. The sensations flashing through her felt right, and also wrong. There was an immovable wedge between them. Unresolved hurt and betrayal that might never heal.

The silence grew as they strolled past the livery and lumber mill, toward the school. Stopping by the creek, he made no move to sit on the bench.

"Noah made the bench years ago," he explained. "It's a favorite for locals."

Instead of responding, she tugged her arm free, taking the few steps to the edge of the water. "I don't know what it is about rolling water, but it always draws me."

"It's soothing." His warm breath washed across her cheek as his hands settled on her waist. "I come here often. Someday, we'll ride to my cabin. There's a creek not fifty feet away. I can hear it at night."

Unbidden, Shane's body reacted to their closeness. The knot of longing lodged in his chest grew, wishing their lives hadn't been torn apart.

Leaning her back against his chest, she sighed. "If I'm still here."

His fingers tightened on her waist, forcing himself to stay calm. "You already have plans to leave?"

"Not yet."

He let the answer settle in, wondering at the meaning.

"There is a great deal to discuss before I make plans to leave."

She'd beat him to it. His reasons for the walk were to learn the truth about her leaving, and understand why Angela had never tried to contact him.

Stepping back, he took her hand in his. "Then we should resume our walk."

Returning to the boardwalk, Shane led her toward the church, tipping his hat at people he knew. He stopped a few times for him to introduce her, then continued. Walking around the church, he entered the building in back, closing the door behind them.

"What is this?"

"Our community building. This and the St. James are where a good number of townsfolk and ranchers stayed last Christmas during the blizzard."

Angela's eyes grew wide. "All night?"

"All night. There's a kitchen in the back. We brought extra blankets from the hotel. It was quite an experience. Do you want to sit down?"

She spotted the chairs, but shook her head. "I'd rather stand, or continue walking."

His response was a crisp nod. "All right." Holding out his hand, she slipped her fingers through his.

Outside, they walked past the new boardinghouse. Minutes passed in silence before Angela spoke.

"I have never been as strong as you, Shane."

"You're four years younger, sheltered by your father."

"Please don't make excuses for me." Catching her bottom lip between her teeth, her fingers tightened on his, fighting for courage. "A few days after you asked him for my hand, Pa woke me early. He said my aunt and uncle in Boston sent money for train fare. I thought he meant him,

Ma, and I would all be going for a visit. He refused to let me run to your house, or send a message."

Angela's chest squeezed at what she'd learned later was a life altering betrayal. "Pa drove the wagon, Ma by his side. You already know she was never a strong woman. I don't believe she ever went against him."

"And not that day," Shane muttered.

She shook her head. "No, not that day. He put me on the train at the last minute, told me to find three seats. By the time I realized what he'd done, the train was pulling away from the station."

Hearing her voice crack, he glanced down at her, seeing a lone tear slide down her cheek. Using his other hand, he swiped it away with the pad of his thumb.

"You don't have to tell me anymore today, Angie."

Choking out a laugh, she touched his arm. "I want you to know the entire story. Is there some place we can talk where we'd have privacy?"

Scanning the street, his gaze landed on Ruby's. She'd open soon, although there'd be few customers for several hours.

"I know just the place." Clutching Angie's hand, he steered her down the street.

Chapter Eighteen

"Why, Deputy Banderas. I don't often see you in here so early. And who is that with you?" Ruby ushered them inside.

Removing his hat and stepping aside, Shane smiled down at Angie. "Miss Ruby, this is Miss Angela Baldwin. Angie, this is Miss Ruby, owner of the Grand Palace."

Holding out her hand, Angela gasped when Ruby drew her into a hug. "If you're a friend of Shane's, then you're family. You two looking for a little privacy?"

"A table where we can talk in private, Ruby."

"As you can see, we have plenty of them. How about over there?" Ruby waved a hand to a private table along the back wall.

Bending, Shane brushed a kiss across the woman's cheek. "It's perfect. I'll take a whiskey when you have a chance." He looked at Angela.

"Do you have sarsaparilla?"

A wide grin broke across Ruby's face. "I sure do. One of the girls will be right over with your drinks. Get comfortable, I'll make certain no one bothers you."

Placing a hand on the small of her back, they crossed the distance to their table. "Is this all right with you, Angie?"

"Quiet and private. It's perfect." Placing a palm against her chest, she pressed, hoping to quiet the erratic pounding of her heart. Determined to finish without further tears, she inhaled a slow breath, letting it out in a gentle flow.

A curvy, red haired woman appeared with two glasses, and a shameless smile for Shane. "A whiskey for the deputy and a sarsaparilla for the lady. Will there be anything else?" A wink accompanied the question.

"Nothing else," Shane answered, never taking his focus off Angela. Picking up his glass, he took a sip, not wanting to rush her.

Grasping her glass with both hands, she stared into the light golden soft drink. "When I realized the Winslows meant to keep me in Boston, I tried sending a letter to you. Mr. Winslow called me to his study the same afternoon. He told me I wasn't allowed to send letters to anyone except my family." She choked out a bitter laugh. "He made it clear there'd be consequences if I disobeyed him."

Eyes full of regret, Angela looked at Shane. "I should've kept trying, found a way to get a letter to you." Staring back into the drink, she shook her head. "I was a coward."

He didn't try to touch her, nor offer words of encouragement. Taking another sip of whiskey, Shane rested his arms on the table. Again, he waited.

"After a while, I made myself believe you'd forgotten me, found someone else."

"Even though I was told you died, I never forgot you, Angie."

Rubbing a hand over her forehead, she fixed her gaze on the piano across the room. "They treated me as a part of their house staff, but also as a member of their family. There were times I'd accompany them to social functions. A few days later, I'd be left behind. I didn't care. My preference was to stay away from their friends."

Lifting her glass, she took a long swallow, her mind going to Carson. Her friend and protector, the man she'd agreed to marry. She'd found Shane again because of him.

"Mr. Winslow encouraged the engagement to his son. I never understood why he was so adamant we marry." Angela lifted her face, meeting Shane's impassive gaze. "We were good friends, cared about each other, but not in love. Carson went along with his father's wishes. We became engaged not long before Mr. Winslow suffered a heart attack. He died a few days later."

Shane's brow lifted. "Carson didn't end the engagement?"

"No. If anything, he was even more committed to a shared life with me. It was during this time Carson made plans for our trip west. You know the rest."

Shane rolled the glass between his fingers before swallowing the last of the amber liquid. Setting the glass down, he continued to watch it. A thoughtful stare, as if pondering something important. Perhaps life changing.

"Why did your father send you to Boston?" He leaned closer. "Why would the Winslows accept you into their home?"

Angela shied away from his intense glare, clutching her hands in her lap. Recalling the document she'd found in Edith Winslow's belongings after the woman's death, she touched her reticule, knowing the explanation Shane sought was inside.

The entry door to their right flew open. Two young men hesitated, allowing their eyes to adjust to the darkness before entering. Glancing around, their gazes locked on Angela. Both men touched the brims of their hats, giving a slight bow before moving toward a table at the center of the Palace.

Shane recognized them, but didn't know their names. "Do you know those men?"

"Not really. Martha and I met them after leaving the bookstore. As I recall, their names are Cal Rivers and Jeb Franklin. Why?"

He didn't answer as he studied them from their spot at the back. Both wore six-shooters low on their hips, the same as many gunslingers. Although dressed as ranch hands, the way they walked, their manner, told a different story.

"I suppose they inquired as to escorting you and Martha to breakfast, or lunch." Shane's voice held an unintended edge.

Lifting her chin, her eyes didn't flinch when meeting his accusing gaze. "Yes, although I had no intention of accepting their invitation." She noticed the hard lines of his face relax.

"What you do with your time isn't my business, Angie."

"I'd hoped you'd believe otherwise." The comment had his brows drawing together. "I'm certainly interested in your private life, Deputy Banderas." Her eyes twinkled with mirth.

A small smile curved his lips. "You are?" Reaching under the table, he took her hand in his. "There's not much to my life, private or otherwise."

Enjoying the warmth of his hand, Angela tried not to hope it meant more than a casual touch between friends. Were they still friends? She didn't have an answer. "Mine either."

Thinking back on what he'd said a few days earlier, Angela forced herself to ask the question which had bothered her.

"You said there was a woman you wanted to pursue." Her voice wavered, bottom lip quivering. "Is that true?"

Shane knew what she asked. "At the time, yes, I did have someone in mind."

"Oh." She pulled her hand from his, feeling foolish for believing it meant something. "Do you mind if we leave?" Starting to stand, she stilled at his soft request.

"Don't leave, Angie."

"If your heart is somewhere else, you shouldn't be here with me."

"I still have questions," he coaxed.

"The answers don't matter if there's another woman." Stomach in a knot, she shoved back her chair. "Martha will be wondering where I am."

Standing, he wrapped an arm around her waist, pulling her against him. "There's a woman I've considered courting. Your arrival changed my plans." He shrugged.

"The nurse. Carrie something."

"Stop it, Angie. This isn't about Carrie or any other woman. It's about you and me, and if we have any hope of a future."

Before she could respond, he moved his hands to cup her face, lowering his mouth. It was a soft kiss, not chaste, not heated. Lifting his head, he searched her eyes before glancing around. Confirming no one watched, he captured her lips again, this one deeper, more passionate.

Shane knew they had to stop. Even if they were somewhat hidden in the back, too many people were around, including Ruby. The woman didn't miss much.

Ending the kiss, he stared into her glassy eyes for a moment before straightening. "Have lunch with me, Angie. Martha is welcome to join us."

Touching her face, feeling the heat course through her, she nodded. "Lunch would be nice."

Leaning down, he lowered his voice. "You're the only woman I'm interested in, Angie."

"What if my answers to your questions aren't what you want to hear?"

Stroking his fingers down her cheek, he followed them with a brush of his lips. "We'll deal with it then." Tossing money on the table, he took her hand. "Come on."

~~~

Shane sat across the desk from Gabe, Harley in a chair next to him. Even though important, their meeting wasn't as enjoyable as his lunch with Angela and Martha earlier.

Gabe leaned forward, his voice soothing. "How long since you've seen your father, Harley?"

Staring at his hands, Harley bit his lower lip. "A long time. Ma says he's gone."

"Did she tell you where?"

Shaking his head, the young man didn't meet Gabe's penetrating gaze. "No. He's just gone."

"Did Sheriff Sterling tell you why you're with us in Splendor?"

"Ma told me she was sending me on a trip." His eyes lit with excitement. "I get to work with horses."

Chuckling, Gabe leaned back. "Yes, you do. Deputy Banderas and I will take you to the ranch tomorrow."

Brows scrunching, his face twisted in confusion. "Can it be Deputy Shane?"

"Sheriff Gabe means me, partner."

Harley's smile transformed his features. Again, he pointed at Shane. "We're partners."

"Yes, we are."

Glancing out the window, Harley jumped up, running to it. Staring, he turned toward Shane and Gabe, bouncing on the balls of his feet. "I don't like those men." He whirled to look back outside.

Joining him at the window, Shane looked up and down the boardwalk. "Which men?"

Harley ran outside, stopping a few feet from the door. "Those men." He pointed at two men standing outside Finn's.

Shane recognized them. Cal Rivers and Jeb Franklin, the men who invited Angela and Martha to share a meal with them.

"Why don't you like them?"

Harley's expression turned solemn. "They rob banks."

"How do you know?"

"I heard them talking about taking money from banks. I don't think they saw me." Shaking his head, Harley continued to watch the men until they disappeared inside the saloon. "I don't like them."

"Come back inside. I need you to tell Gabe what you told me."

Harley didn't stop talking for fifteen minutes, explaining to the sheriff what he'd already told Shane.

"This couldn't have been here in Splendor," Shane said under his breath.

Harley shook his head. "Big Pine."

"Do you know which bank?" Gabe asked.

Nodding, he lifted his arms. "The big bank. The one at the end of town."

Shane shot a look at Gabe before asking one more question. "The one close to the stage station?"

A huge smile lifted the corners of Harley's mouth. "Yes!"

Chapter Nineteen

"Cal and Jeb haven't come back, boss."

Rand Sutton glared at one of the men who'd robbed the bank in Big Pine, unable to hide his disdain. "You think I don't know that? They were supposed to be back days ago."

Rubbing a hand over his thinning hair, Rand paced away from the camp. His men had pulled off the plan suggested by Cal and Jeb without a flaw. He'd stayed hidden half a mile east of town, relieved when his men returned, bags of money clutched in several hands.

Watching behind them until certain no one followed, Sutton motioned his men toward a trail heading north. Narrow, taking them through large boulders and thick brush, they rode for an hour before stopping at a closed tunnel. An abandoned mine. Gold, Rand believed.

For two days, they remained northeast of town before returning to their previous camp, where he expected Cal and Jeb to join them. There'd been no sign of them.

"What do you want to do, boss? The boys are getting restless."

Rand fought to tap down the anger aimed at the man who'd followed him from camp. He wanted to lash out, knowing he had to rein in his temper before saying something he'd regret.

The man was jumpy, as were the rest of the gang. They'd wanted to ride out when realizing Cal and Jeb weren't waiting for them. Rand preferred to wait. Those boys were his best.

The sound of approaching horses had both men drawing their revolvers. Slipping behind a broad tree trunk, Rand crouched, his six-shooter aimed in front of him. Ready to fire, he held up at the last moment, recognizing Cal and Jeb.

Reining to a stop in front of Rand and the other outlaw, the two slid to the ground, prepared for their boss's wrath. Sutton didn't holster his gun as he stepped to within a foot of them.

"Where the hell have you two been?"

Cal swiped a sleeve across his forehead. "We got here as soon as we could. It took longer to get the information on the deputies."

"But you got it?"

Jeb nodded. "More than what you ordered."

Not bothering to hide his excitement, Rand slid the six-shooter into its holster. "What did you learn?"

Grabbing his canteen, Cal took a long, slow swallow of water before handing it to Jeb. When both drank their fill, Cal hung it around his saddlehorn. The two spent the next half an hour describing the town's layout, location of the jail, and number of deputies.

"You're certain Shane Banderas is in Splendor?"

Both men nodded, Cal answering. "The deputy is there, boss."

A feral smile twisted Sutton's face. "He's a deputy. Even better."

Jeb waited for him to say something about the women, letting out a relieved breath when Rand began talking about robbing the bank in Splendor.

"We'll relieve the town of their money and leave several deputies dead, including Banderas. His death will be by my hand."

"Of course, boss," Jeb answered. "Everyone knows he's yours." His shoulders slumped at Sutton's next question.

"I want Banderas's woman. Have you been able to confirm who she is?"

"Not yet." Cal shot a warning look at Jeb. "There are two women sharing a house. Either one could be who you want. We'll head back at first light. It shouldn't take long to learn which one belongs to Banderas."

Rubbing his chin, Rand's narrowed gaze seemed to say more than his words. "You've got two days to get the information to me. One rides back while the other stays close to her. Don't want her to disappear without taking part in my plan."

Jeb lifted a brow. "Your plan?"

An odd cackle burst from Sutton's throat. "She's not just going to watch Banderas die. She's going to be the one to pull the trigger."

Splendor

Angela's arm laced through his could almost convince Shane this was the way it should be. He and the woman he'd loved since they were children. Together, with a bright future before them. Yet he couldn't quite make himself believe it.

His trust in Angela had suffered when learning she hadn't died but had been very much alive. Watching his fellow deputies with their women, others falling in love and marrying, had given him hope. One day, he wanted what they had.

Carrie Galloway had interested him from the first time they'd met. Pretty, smart, with a calm manner he associated with her career as a nurse. They'd eaten in Suzanne's boarding restaurant on several occasions, her with friends, him with fellow deputies.

He'd watched her, heard her uninhibited laughter more than once. Laughter which made him smile, made him want to learn more about her. Shane hadn't missed her sly glances, careful perusal of him. He had no doubt Carrie was as interested in him as he was in her.

Then Angela had walked back into his life. It wasn't intentional. She hadn't been seeking him. Carson Winslow, her fiancé, had accompanied her west. Even after Carson's death, the fact she'd loved another man enough to agree to marriage still hung between them. A tangible hurt he hadn't been able to reconcile. He hoped spending more time with her, learning about the years they'd been apart, would help.

"Where are we walking, Shane?"

So like the Angela of his youth. Always curious, wanting answers. The same as him.

"Nowhere in particular. After such a delicious supper, a walk felt right. Would you rather I escort you back to your house?"

"Not at all. It's a beautiful night, and there's no one else I'd rather be with." She squeezed his arm. "I suppose you still have questions."

"A few."

"Would it be all right if we sat on the bench? I'll answer what I can."

Shane changed directions toward the bench. "What you can?"

"I don't know everything about why my father sent me to the Winslows, or why they took me in." Angela's voice was flat, laced with sadness. "After Edith Winslow, Carson's mother, died, I was charged with going through her personal items. I found information that answered some questions, but raised others."

Reaching the bench, she withdrew her arm to face him. "I know there's another woman in your thoughts. If you love her, if you've already decided she's who you want, please don't make me go through this." Her voice wavered on the last. Still, she held her head high, lifted. It felt as if he'd been punched in the gut.

"Angie..."

"Martha and I will board tomorrow's stage, leaving you to the future you want."

Grabbing her shoulders, his deep green eyes bored into her. "I don't want you to leave."

"But you aren't certain you want me to stay, are you, Shane?"

Dropping his hands, he motioned for her to sit down on the bench. "I'm not certain what I want. Hearing the rest of the story, the reason you were sent to Boston, would help me make a decision."

Eyes flashing in pain, she gave a curt nod. "Between me and Carrie, correct?" Crossing her arms, she moved several steps away. "If you are already in love with her, then no more conversation is necessary. What I found in Edith's belongings is going to make me appear less desirable to you."

Tears burned at the back of her eyes. Tears she refused to let fall. When he didn't respond, she turned back toward town. From here, she could see Noah's saddlery. Had it been less than a week since she and Shane had their confrontation? He'd made it known she had no business being in Splendor. Why hadn't she believed him, continuing the trip to San Francisco?

The answer was simple. She loved him.

Snatching her hand, Shane drew her close enough to sweep a strand of light blonde hair from her face. "I'm not ready for the evening to end. If you are, then I'll walk you home." Brushing a soft kiss across her cheek, he tugged her into his arms. "After all this time, I've never stopped loving you, Angie."

"And Carrie?"

Resting his chin on her head, he tightened his hold. "There are no feelings other than respect. She's a good woman, one who'd make any man an excellent wife. Do I love her? No. Am I curious about whether she and I could make a future together? A little." Feeling her shoulders slump under his hold, he lifted her chin with a finger, placing a warm kiss on her lips. "Understand, I'm not curious enough about Carrie to act on it." With Angela back in his arms, the image of a future with any other woman faded.

"I doubt what else you'll tell me will change my mind about loving you. The hesitancy isn't about the motives of your father and the Winslows."

Her voice lowered to a whisper. "It's about trust."

Shane supposed it did come down to that one word. "You're a wealthy woman, Angie. You could live in a mansion overlooking the Pacific Ocean, have any man you wanted. I'm a small town deputy who has no plans to leave Splendor."

Giving a slow nod, she moved to the bench, taking a seat at one end. "Do you remember the time we walked all the way to the small lake a mile from our homes?"

Sitting next to her, he reached out, covering her hand with his. "I remember."

"The times you and I spent together, talking about our future, are the most precious to me. Do you understand?"

His brows knit together as he shook his head.

"The wealth, what money can buy, doesn't mean much to me. I've always wanted a life with you, Shane. I've dreamed of it. The life we talked about on our walks."

Chest squeezing, he wanted to get down on one knee, ask her to marry him and fulfill her dream. Something held him back. Maybe it was trust. So easy to lose. So difficult to earn back.

Shane wondered if he was putting all the blame for her disappearance on Angela. She hadn't been a willing participant in the separation between them. Her father and the senior Winslow were the ones who stole their future.

Watching the change of emotions on his face, Angela's heart pounded within her chest. "Perhaps sharing what I learned will help you understand. But..."

Seeing the fear on her face, his features softened. "Tell me, Angie. We'll decide what to do from there."

Opening her reticule, she drew out the document. Fearing Shane's reaction, Angela worked to control her erratic breathing, wanting to at least give the pretense of calm. From his expression, she had failed.

Unfolding the paper, she held it with both hands, staring at the first paragraph. She'd read it a hundred times, never quite believing it, knowing Edith's words were true.

Hands shaking, she opened her mouth, then closed it, her gaze darting between Shane and the paper. He didn't question her hesitation, waiting for her to speak.

Inhaling a deep breath, she let it out, searching for the courage required to share the document's contents.

"Ma and Pa are not my real parents."

Chapter Twenty

Shock registered on Shane's face, his features pinched. "The Baldwins aren't your real parents?"

Without answering, Angela held the paper out to him. Slipping it from her fingers, he read, glancing up every few sentences before returning to Edith's handwritten note. He read it a second time, slower, so as not to miss anything. When finished, he lowered the paper to his lap, studying her.

"Do you believe what Edith wrote?"

Angela rubbed her left temple before nodding. "She had no reason to lie. Edith kept it hidden in her bedroom."

Scooting closer, Shane draped an arm over her shoulders, providing what comfort he could. "Do you think Carson knew the truth?"

Leaning into him, she took the solace he offered. "He never mentioned knowing. Wouldn't you think he would have if he knew?"

"Maybe. My instincts tell me he did."

Angela let the comment settle in, acknowledging Shane was right. "Yes, he almost certainly did."

Edith's note, more of a long journal entry, revealed her second cousin, Marie, was Angela's mother. She'd been sixteen when entering into an affair with an older, married man. The pregnancy had come soon afterward. Marie didn't want the baby, had tried to get rid of it.

Somehow, Edith had discovered her cousin's situation. Married a few short months, she'd insisted Marie move into their home. Before the birth, several discussions with the Winslows' pastor resulted in locating a childless couple willing to adopt the baby for a payment of several hundred dollars.

Marie didn't survive the delivery. The doctors had been unable to control the bleeding. They saved the baby, but not the mother. A week later, the Baldwins had left the hospital with a baby girl, moving out of Massachusetts soon afterward.

"I was sold to the Baldwins," she whispered against his shoulder. "Sold, Shane."

Tugging her closer, his hand stroked her arm. "Yes."

Her voice turned thick. "My real mother didn't want me. Neither did her family. The Winslows couldn't wait to get rid of me."

"They came after you when you turned eighteen," Shane reminded her.

"Because the Baldwins demanded more money."

"The document made it sound as if they'd provided funds to the Baldwins every month."

"Yes, but this was different. The Baldwins threatened to reveal the truth, ruin the Winslows' social standing. Instead, the Winslows provided a thousand dollars for their silence and moved me to Boston." She moved a few inches away, looking up at Shane. "They were afraid I'd learn the truth and demand my rightful place in the family."

He nodded. "That is the way it reads, sweetheart." They both stilled at the endearment, Shane recovering first. Kissing the top of her head, he reached over, taking her hand in his.

"I always wondered why my appearance was so different from my ma...from the Baldwins."

"You're so much prettier." He chuckled, hoping to lighten the mood. Her quiet laughter told him it had.

"If they'd told me earlier..." Her voice trailed off for a moment. "I have so many questions. Now there's no one left to answer them." Straightening, she pressed her lips together. "Do the circumstances of my birth, what the Winslows and Baldwins did, bother you?"

Shane's intense gaze met hers. "Of course it bothers me."

Angela stiffened against him. Trying to shove out of his grasp, he tightened his hold.

"Their actions, how you were treated, infuriates me, Angie. You were a sweet, wonderful girl, who matured into a beautiful, smart woman. Any parents would be proud of you."

"Not the Baldwins. They wanted me for the money. That's why the Winslow inheritance means so little to me, Shane."

Eyes flashing as her meaning became clear, he stood, pulling her up in front of him. Wrapping his arms around her waist, he drew her flush against him. Before she understood his intentions, he claimed her mouth.

Her hands moved up his arms, feeling the muscles of his chest. When she wrapped her arms around his neck, he deepened the kiss.

Shane didn't want to let her go, knowing they couldn't continue. Lifting his head, his forehead rested against hers, their breathing thick and uneven.

"I should walk you home."

Angela closed her eyes for an instant to clear her head before stepping out of his arms. "Yes."

"Will you and Martha have lunch with me tomorrow?" He took her hand.

A tentative smile formed on her face, although joy radiated throughout her body. "We'd love to have lunch with you."

Bending, he kissed her again. "I'll come by about eleven."

"Why don't we meet you at the restaurant?" Allowing him to lead her away from the creek, her smile grew.

"If you don't mind, I'd rather come for you, Angie."

"That would be wonderful, Shane."

Shane laid in bed longer than usual the following morning, attempting to sort out all he'd learned the night before. Edith's detailed explanation answered many questions, helping Angela understand an astonishing past.

What it didn't answer was why she'd found it so hard to get a message to him. She'd had years to sneak out a letter, or give it to a friend, perhaps Martha, to mail for her. Yes, he'd left within months of her leaving, but he'd communicated with his parents several times a year, made certain they knew how to reach him.

If their situations had been reversed, Shane would've done anything, stopped at nothing, to get word to Angela. She'd given up after a single attempt.

The knowledge ate at him, tore at his heart. As much as he still loved her, craved a future together, he couldn't move past the fact she'd let him go with such ease.

How long would it take him to move past the loss of trust? He wondered if Angela had returned to Splendor because she had no reason to stay in Boston. Shane was a link to her past, a man who'd once loved her, had never broken a promise. A man who would've done anything for her.

Flinging off the blanket, he swung his legs to the floor, bending at the waist. His hands grasped the sides of his head, pressing to relieve the growing ache. He kept packets of headache powder, refusing to use one this morning. Shane figured a few cups of coffee and breakfast would take care of the incessant pounding.

Dressing, he walked straight to McCall's, taking a seat near the back. Waiting to order until drinking a cup of coffee, he spoke little to Betts, chowing down on four eggs, six slices of bacon, and thick toast. His headache had subsided, allowing him to consider what to do about Angela.

Stepping into the mid-morning sun, he glanced up and down the street as the hairs on his neck prickled. His stomach tightened, instincts on alert. Watching for nothing in particular, Shane sensed a threat.

His first thought was of Angela. Hurrying along the boardwalk, he had no intention of stopping for anything until Stan Petermann waved him down. Impatient, he waved back, pretending to misinterpret the man's desire to talk.

"Morning, Deputy. You got a minute?"

He didn't, but couldn't ignore Stan's plea. "What can I do for you?"

Motioning him inside, the owner of Petermann's General Store walked straight to the storeroom. "Look at this." He indicated the broken handle on the back door.

Dropping to a knee, Shane studied the knob on both sides. "Appears someone tried to get into your store. Do you remember locking it last night?"

"Sure did. Checked it twice before leaving."

Standing, Shane looked over the shelves stacked with goods for the front of the store. "Anything missing?" He didn't know how anyone could tell with the number of different items.

"Two blankets, half a dozen apples, and a few cans of beans. People trying to stay warm while filling their bellies."

Shane shoved his hat off his forehead. "What about money?"

"I take it with me at night. Not much, as I deposit most of it at the bank in the late afternoon."

"I'll let Gabe know, Stan. He'll have deputies check the store several times at night. Are you going to be able to fix the handle before you leave?"

Stan waved him off. "I've got an extra in the back. Means I'll need to order a spare from Noah."

"All right. I'd best get to the jail."

"Hello, Deputy Banderas."

The pleasant voice had him turning while removing his hat. "Miss Galloway." He couldn't stop the smile tipping up the corners of his mouth. "You look fetching this morning."

Her laugh filled the store. "It's a plain blue dress, Deputy. Nothing fancy."

Looking her over, he shook his head. "Then I guess it must be you."

They continued an easy banter, neither noticing the woman entering the store. After a couple minutes, Carrie stepped closer.

"I hope I'm not being too forward, but would you care to join me for supper sometime soon, Deputy."

He thought of Angela, his stomach twisting. Shane liked Carrie, didn't want to embarrass her in front of Stan. "How about you being my guest for breakfast?"

Her eyes sparked in anticipation. "That would be wonderful."

"I'll come by the clinic soon."

Carrie's exuberant smile enchanted him. Still, he had a commitment to Angela. At least until they discovered if there was a chance at a future.

Surprising him, she lifted onto her toes, placing a kiss on his cheek. "Thank you. I'll look forward to it."

Feeling his face heat, he tipped his hat as she walked out the front door. Following her, Shane didn't notice Angela an aisle away, mouth open, features twisted in painful disbelief.

"You're certain it was Shane?" Martha refused to believe he had invited another woman to breakfast.

Pouring a cup of fresh coffee, Angela cradled it in her hands, leaning against the kitchen counter. "It was definitely Shane. The woman was Carrie Galloway."

"Isn't that..." Martha's voice trailed off, a bitter taste in her mouth.

"The woman he intended to court. It seems he still holds an interest in her. After last night, I thought we were working toward a possible future. It seems I was wrong."

Martha stepped closer, touching her arm. "I'm sure you must've misunderstood."

Moving to a chair at the kitchen table, she sat down, the joy of last night disappearing at what she'd seen and heard. "No misunderstanding. Before leaving, she kissed him on the cheek."

"What? Well, if that's the kind of woman she is, he can have her."

Angela bristled at her friend's protective nature. She hoped Shane didn't stop by early or Martha just might take a pan to him.

Several moments passed as Angela accepted what she'd witnessed. Unable to deny he wasn't as committed to her as she was to him, she considered what to do next.

"You aren't still going to lunch with him, are you?"

"It would be impolite not to, Martha."

"Impolite? Well, I'm not going. Although, I wouldn't mind seeing you tear into him."

"There will be no tearing." She chuckled without a hint of humor.

Angela had to clear her head, decide what to say. Determination took hold.

She'd have lunch with Shane, and by the time the meal ended, she'd know his intentions toward her, and toward Carrie Galloway.

Chapter Twenty-One

Shane continued his second turn around town, his mind bouncing between three people. Rand Sutton, Angela, and Carrie. He felt a pang of guilt knowing he had no business thinking about the last, or inviting her to breakfast.

True, no date had been set, yet he'd led her on. He made a decision, one he should've made that morning. After lunch with Angela, he'd go straight to the clinic and apologize. If she'd let him, Shane would explain.

Finding himself on Rimrock Street, he pulled out his grandfather's pocket watch. Close to eleven, the time he'd agreed to call on Angela. He squelched the ripple of excitement. It would do him no good to believe they had a future before understanding her failure to contact him during her years in Boston.

He should talk to Hawke.

They'd begun their deputy jobs in Splendor within days of each other, becoming fast friends. Before Hawke married Beauty, they'd shared the house Shane still occupied. It was too big for one person, hence the purchase of Noah's cabin.

Most of his belongings were already in the comfortable home on Sunrise Ridge. Not that he owned much. A few shirts and a pair of pants were still in the wardrobe at the house in town. He hadn't quite been able to finalize the move. Shane knew the reason.

Angela had arrived in town as he'd closed the purchase with Noah. It had been recorded at the land office and loan documents signed at the bank. To celebrate, he and Noah had walked to the Dixie for a round of drinks. Afterward, Shane had made the decision to court Carrie, as if she'd already shown an interest. Thinking of it now, he winced at his arrogance.

He now understood why he'd held back approaching Carrie. Angela was about to reenter his life.

Seeing her house up ahead, he frowned at the sight of two men leaning against the back wall of Caleb Covington's house. A fellow deputy with a wife and son, he was another of Shane's friends. Rumor had it, he and May were trying for another child.

Growing closer, Shane recognized the two men. Not that he'd met them, but Angela and Martha had. Both had the look of gunslingers. He hated them on sight.

Stomping his boots on the bottom step of her porch, he nodded at the men before reaching the front door. Two quick raps and Angela stood before him. His breath caught at her beauty. Then he noticed her bland expression.

"You look lovely."

Angela offered a hint of a smile before picking up her reticule. "I'm ready."

Glancing over her shoulder, he inclined his head inside. "Is Martha coming with us?"

"She's not feeling well."

Shane heard the lack of inflection in Angela's voice, the absence of anticipation at spending lunch with him. He wondered what had changed since last night. Walking past him, she took the steps to the street.

The two outlaws were gone. That was how Shane now thought of them. For a blink, the image of an angry, menacing Rand Sutton flashed in his head. The threat still hung over him, which meant it threatened his fellow deputies, and anyone close to him. If the murderer found out about Angela, he might try to use her against Shane.

Holding out his arm, she hesitated a moment before sliding hers through it. She didn't lean into him as she had the night before. Walking to Suzanne's boardinghouse, his confusion mounted at her lingering silence.

"Are you feeling well, Angie?"

"Why do you ask?"

Answering a question with a question had never been her style. "You're quiet is all. After last night..." He quieted as they crossed the street to the restaurant's front entrance. Stepping onto the boardwalk, he stopped, turning to face her. "You seem distracted."

Forcing a small smile, she slid her arm from his. "Would it be all right to put off this discussion until ordering lunch? I'm famished." Her attempt at humor failed.

"We'll select our meals, then talk." Opening the door, Angela walked inside, smiling at an approaching Suzanne. A smile he hadn't seen since the night before.

Their table was in the center of the room. Not Shane's favorite location, though he didn't complain. One table remained, and it was close to theirs. The others were filled with people talking and laughing. Other than a brief nod from those who recognized him, they were left alone.

Angela didn't look at him as they ordered. Sipping coffee with milk and sugar, she glanced around, as if seeking an escape. She surprised him by meeting his gaze.

"How did your morning walk around town go, Shane? Anything exciting?"

Searching her face, he thought of the morning. "Someone broke into the general store last night. Stan arrived to find the handle on the back door broken."

"What was taken?"

"Blankets and food. I spoke with Stan, then told Gabe about what I saw. Both believe it's a couple older children they've seen around town."

"Someone's cold and starving."

Shane nodded. "Gabe got Stan's approval to let it go, for now. He'll increase the number of times deputies pass by at night." Shrugging, he swallowed more coffee.

Angela did the same, setting down her cup. "Nothing besides the theft at the general store. A quiet morning."

Suzanne placed their meals down before refilling their cups. "Let me know if you want dessert. I have berry pie and a beautiful chocolate cake May Covington made."

Caleb's wife worked as a dessert and pastry chef at the Eagle's Nest. As a part owner with Nick, Gabe, and Lena

Evan's, May provided her baked goods to the boardinghouse.

Shane looked at Angela, who shook her head. "I'll have a slice of cake, Suzanne."

"I'll set one aside for you." Suzanne walked off, leaving them alone.

He tucked into his meal, noticing Angela moved her food around, eating little. "I thought you were famished."

Setting down her fork, she let out a deep sigh. "How is Miss Galloway?"

Shane stilled, confusion clouding his features. Angela must've heard about him speaking with Carrie at the general store. Forming a response, his throat constricted at her next words.

"Breakfast was a good decision. Although lunch is nice, also. Supper at her house might've been a little bold. Then again, she must have a great interest in you to make the offer."

"Angie..."

"She's a very pretty woman, Shane. Your attraction to her is understandable. I'd hoped you would wait to show your interest in her until we had a chance to, well..." She stared at her lap. "After last night, I thought..."

"Let me explain."

Shaking her head, she placed her napkin on the table, meaning to stand. "There's no need. I was in the store. You were so smitten with her, you never noticed me."

Standing, he walked around the table, bending down. "It isn't what you think."

A pained chuckle answered his comment. Reaching out, she cupped his jaw. "It's all right, Shane. You were honest with me about wanting to court her. I should've understood that no matter what happened between us, you still planned to court her."

He leaned into the warmth of her palm, ignoring the curious glances of others in the restaurant. "I'm not courting her, Angie. Please, come outside with me and I'll explain."

Lowering her hand, tears burned at the back of her eyes. She didn't want to cause a scene or make life harder for Shane. Angela doubted there was much he could say. After all, she'd heard the conversation, seen the expectant look in his eyes. Carrie meant something to him, whether he'd admit it to Angela or not.

She'd already been considering plans to leave Splendor. Staying wouldn't be possible. Watching him court and marry another woman would destroy her. Angela thought of Carson, and how Shane must've felt about her engagement to another man. Until now, she hadn't considered what he'd gone through.

"All right."

Standing, he helped her up before digging into a pocket. Placing money on the table, he took her elbow. Once outside, he dropped his hand.

"We'll go to my house. It's quiet, and no one will bother us." When she didn't object, he took her hand, slipping it through his arm.

Taking the quickest route to his house, he ushered her inside. Closing the door, Shane nodded toward a chair. "I don't have much to offer you. Most of my stuff is at the cabin. I could stoke the fire and make coffee."

Walking around, she poked her head into one bedroom, then another. It was much the same as the house she shared with Martha.

"I don't want anything." She didn't sit down, finding it easier to stand. Aware of him watching her, she walked into the kitchen, deciding to lean against the counter.

Shane kept his distance, not happy with the desolation on her face. His thoughtless conversation with Carrie had caused her discomfort, making her doubt him. The same as she'd caused his doubts about her.

"Carrie came into the store while I was talking to Stan. You don't know him well, but he's one of the worst gossips in town. When he and I were finished, Stan hung around, listening to my conversation with Carrie."

Crossing her arms, she gave a slow nod, her features rigid. Eyes flat, she didn't make a sound.

"Her invitation to supper surprised me. With Stan listening, I wasn't going to humiliate her by refusing. Suggesting breakfast was my way of making it less personal, and not embarrassing her. She's a good woman, Angie. I planned to stop by the clinic after lunch to explain about you and me. How we're courting, and having a meal with her wouldn't be right."

Eyes widening, her mouth opened. "Courting?"

"What do you think this is about? I love you, Angie. You said you love me. In my mind, either of us spending time with someone else isn't going to happen until there's a decision about our future." He walked to within a foot of her, his hands stroking down her arms. "Our shared future, Angie."

Finding it hard to talk, her breathing quickened. "You want a future with me?"

"Why would that surprise you?"

Lips pressed together, her gaze moved over him, praying he was telling the truth. "A little. You believe I gave up getting a letter to you after one attempt. To my shame, it's true. Fear was a constant part of my life after being sent away. Not because of the Winslows, but the fear of being sent away again. It's not an excuse, Shane. I failed us when fear kept me from trying again."

Thinking he understood, believing they could forge a future, his arms wrapped around her. "I've always wished you were still in my life, Angie. Always. Even when I thought you'd died, the dream of us together wouldn't die."

Wrapping her arms around his waist, she hung on, as if letting go wasn't an option. It wasn't, for either of them.

"What about Carrie?"

Resting his chin on the top of her head, he breathed in the sweet scent of her hair. "I'll talk to her when we leave." He could feel her nod against his chest. "By evening, everyone in town will know I'm courting you. Will you be happy with that?"

A moment passed before she looked up at him. "Nothing would make me happier."

Chapter Twenty-Two

"We have to get away from here before Rand makes his move. Idaho would be good." Jeb stuffed his saddlebags with provisions, including a bottle of whiskey.

Sutton had insisted they leave the camp with their share of the bank take, even though neither had been on the raid. They hadn't argued.

Riding hard, the two friends had entered Splendor late morning, not bothering to hide their horses. They hadn't intended to stop by Angela's house, glad they had when Banderas showed up.

It had been an easy decision to ignore their boss's orders and leave the couple alone. If Rand wanted the man dead, the woman kidnapped, he'd have to do it without their help.

"A drink at the Dixie, then we ride out."

"No, Cal. We need to leave now. I've got a feeling…"

"You have plenty of *feelings*, Jeb. Why's this one different?"

Twitching, he rubbed the back of his neck.

"Hell. Why didn't you tell me you had the twitches?" Tying his rain slicker and bedroll behind the saddle, Cal swung atop his gelding. Jeb did the same. The last anyone in Splendor saw of them was dirt kicking up around their horses.

Hat in hand, Shane entered the clinic, his stomach twisting at the reason for his visit. Closing the front door, he stilled at the sound of soft footfalls on the stairs. He knew it would be Carrie.

A cheerful smile greeted him. "Hello, Deputy. I didn't expect to see you so soon."

Fingering the rim of his hat, he found it hard to return her enthusiastic welcome. "Is there someplace we can talk?"

Smile fading, she motioned to the examination room. "This one would be best."

Leaving the door open, Shane cleared his throat, releasing a forceful breath. "I'm not going to be able to meet you for breakfast. I would've said so at the general store if Stan wasn't huddling so close as to hear us."

Brows furrowing, she tilted her head. "I'm not sure I understand."

He hadn't expected her to. "Your invitation for supper surprised me, Carrie. May I call you Carrie?"

"Of course, but only if I may call you Shane."

Nodding, he set his hat on a chair. "Because of Stan's presence, his tendency to spread gossip, I thought it best not to explain my situation to you until later. My invitation should have never been made, Carrie, but I didn't see a way around it with Stan listening."

"I see. Please don't worry about it, Shane."

"If I wasn't already courting someone else…"

Brows lifting, he saw the instant his words penetrated. "Who is the lucky woman?"

"A woman I knew well before moving to Splendor. Her name is Angela Baldwin. I'm sorry, Carrie."

The smile returned. Shane had to admire her ability to take what she must consider rejection with such grace. "It was breakfast, not an invitation for more. If I'd known about Miss Baldwin, I never would've approached you."

He understood, wishing he'd been honest at the general store. "I hope my mishandling of your invitation doesn't prevent us from being friends." Picking up his hat, he was more than ready to leave. Even so, he felt a pang of regret.

"Of course it doesn't. Please think nothing more about it."

Shane left the clinic with a combination of relief and remorse. Carrie would make someone a wonderful wife and mother. It just wouldn't be him.

Settling his hat low on his head, he strode toward the jail, taking time to check each business as he passed. Later, he'd recall being distracted by a possible future with Angela. That was why he missed the man coming up behind him, shoving the barrel of a gun into his back.

"Keep walking, Deputy."

He didn't recognize the throaty voice, which meant it wasn't Sutton. "What do you want?"

Another hard poke into his back answered him. "You'll see."

They reached Grant Street. Chinatown to the townsfolk. Turning down the street, Shane spotted fellow deputy, Cole Santori, talking to the owner of the herb and medicine shop. When Cole raised his hand in greeting, Shane gave a sharp, almost imperceptible, shake of his head.

"Keep walking." The man moved to Shane's side, attempting to conceal his six-shooter from the other deputy.

Neither Shane nor his captor were prepared for Cole's swift action. Drawing his revolver, he aimed, and fired twice, putting one bullet in the man's shoulder, another in his thigh. Splattered with his captor's blood, Shane whirled to face Cole.

"You could've missed."

Cole look down at the wounded man who'd landed face down. "I didn't."

"You were lucky."

"I'm that good, Banderas. Who is he?" Using the tip of his boot, Cole rolled the man over.

Shane knelt down, studying the man. He had a thick beard, and his hair was going gray. "Never seen him before."

"I'm dying. Get me a doctor." The guttural cry didn't affect either man.

"Could be he's one of Sutton's men."

Shaking his head, Shane took in the man's clothes. "He's not dressed as you'd expect for a gunslinger."

The thought had him thinking back to Big Pine, Harley, and his father. He'd never seen a drawing of the older man. Could he have discovered his son was brought to Splendor? If so, how had Dale Sloan recognized him?

Two more deputies, Caleb Covington and Mack Mackey, ran toward them, guns drawn. Dropping to the ground, Caleb checked the man's wounds. Removing his handkerchief, he wrapped it around the man's thigh in an attempt to stop the bleeding. Taking the handkerchief Mack offered, he stuffed it into the shoulder wound.

"Get back so I can take a look at him." Doctor Clay McCord shoved away the deputies. Taking one look, he opened his black satchel. "Who applied the tourniquet?"

"I did," Caleb answered.

"Good work. I'd appreciate if you men would get him to the clinic." McCord noticed Shane's blood splattered clothing. "Were you hit?"

Shaking his head, he leaned down to help up the wounded man. "Not my blood."

Mack shoved Shane away. "We can get this. Go home and clean up. We'll meet you back at the jail."

Taking another look, Shane's gaze narrowed. Even with the contorted features, he could see a resemblance between the man and Harley. Forgetting about cleaning up, he ran to the jail, bursting through the front door.

"What's got you so fired up, Banderas?"

"I think Dale Sloan is at the clinic, Gabe."

Coming to his feet, the sheriff grabbed his hat. "Explain while we walk."

Shane related what had happened in the last twenty minutes. "Santori is a darn good shot. Don't tell him that. If it is Sloan, how would he know I'm the one who brought Harley to Splendor?"

"We're going to find out. Get yourself cleaned up and meet me at the clinic."

Enoch Weaver still resided in one upstairs room at the clinic, recovering from his last heart attack. Doc McCord had said he could go home...if he had someone to stay with him. McCord suggested talking with Ruth Paige, the reverend's wife. The church women might be able to stay with Enoch in shifts. Until then, he was stuck in his small upstairs room at the clinic.

Hearing shouting from downstairs, he tossed off his covers and slid into the slippers Nurse Carrie had given him. Checking the upstairs and finding it empty, he made his way down the stairs with a tight grip on the handrails.

The yelling continued. A man's voice Enoch didn't recognize. Stopping at the last stair, he strained his neck to see into the exam room. Carrie removed the man's blood-soaked shirt before slicing open his right pant leg from hip to ankle. The man protested, quieting when she spoke to him, offering a smile.

"Can you tell me your last name, Mr..."

"Don't matter. Fix me up and I'll be out of here."

"That's up to the doctor, Mr..."

"You aren't going to stop asking until I tell you, are you?"

Carrie gave a short nod. "No, I'm not."

Blowing out a curse, he stared at the ceiling. "Sloan."

"Well, Mr. Sloan, these are serious wounds. It's doubtful the doctor will allow you to leave until he knows you have a place to stay and someone to help you."

"Look, missy, I'll decide when to leave. Not some fancy doctor." He yelped when she opened his pants. The blood had dried, causing his skin to tear.

"Sorry, Mr. Sloan."

Enoch glanced over his shoulder at Doc McCord. "Why are you out of bed?" Clay asked.

"Bored. Heard the yelling and knew Carrie has done all she can do for Sloan."

"Sloan?" Clay asked.

"The man's last name. He told Carrie."

"Why don't you sit down until we're finished with Mr. Sloan? One of us will help you back upstairs when we're finished."

Moving his shaky legs, Enoch walked past the open exam room door, lowering himself onto a chair facing the front windows. Resting his head against the wall, he closed his eyes. They popped open when the front door opened.

"Afternoon, Sheriff."

"Enoch. It's good to see you up and about." Gabe glanced into the exam room a moment before it closed. "Do you know who the doctor is working on?"

"A man named Sloan."

Gabe's eyes sparked for an instant. "Do you know a first name?"

Enoch shook his head.

Leaning back, he stretched out his long legs. It had to be Dale Sloan. He now knew who they would be arresting. "When are you going home?"

"As soon as Doc finds someone to stay with me." He snorted. "He doesn't want me alone. Won't be for long."

Gabe sat next to him. "Why don't you stay with my family? My father is back in town, Jack is old enough to help you, and Lena's home most of the time. We have plenty of room."

Openmouthed, Enoch stared at the sheriff. "I wouldn't want to be a bother."

Gabe set a hand on the older man's shoulder. "No bother at all. I'll make arrangements with Clay. I'm sure you want to get out of here soon."

"Yesterday."

Chuckling, Gabe removed his hand. "We'll get you moved later today."

Slapping his hand on his thighs, Enoch pushed himself up. His shaky legs felt stronger. "I'd better pack so I don't hold you up." Renewed energy carried him upstairs.

Shane came through the door, taking a seat near Gabe. "They still working on him?"

The sheriff nodded. "Enoch says the man's name is Sloan."

Chapter Twenty-Three

Rand loaded six bullets into his revolver, taking aim at the tin cans lined up on a fallen log. Pulling the trigger, one can flew into the air. Following with five more shots, he cursed at the two remaining targets.

Hearing dried branches breaking behind him, he swung around, his six-shooter aimed at the intruder. "What the hell are you doing sneaking up on me? I told you boys not to bother me."

Dave Ball, one of the older gang members, held his arms out, palms open. "We gotta problem, boss."

Holstering the gun, Rand scrubbed a hand down his face. "What problem?"

"Riders coming from the south. They're headed straight toward us."

"Did you get a good look at them?"

"They're soldiers. My guess is they're traveling to Fort Connall up north."

"Or to help the law hunt down the men who robbed the Big Pine bank," Rand mumbled.

Dave's lips pressed together. "We don't have long before they'll be on us."

Their camp was hidden from the main trail north. Staying wasn't worth the chance of the soldiers stumbling across them.

"Let the men know we're riding out."

Dave hesitated a moment. "Which way we going?"

Rand looked around. Early morning, with miles of open space. "We'll stay in the gully, ride east, then south."

Breaking into a run, Dave crossed the distance to their camp far ahead of Rand. By the time he reached the camp, Sutton's men were mounting their horses. A feral grin broke across his face. Someone had already tacked up his gelding.

Riding at a slow pace, so as not to kick up a cloud of dirt, they covered five miles before Sutton motioned for them to stop. "Dave, see if you can spot anyone following."

Dismounting, he pulled field glasses from his saddlebag, crawling up to the top of the gully. Careful, so as not to give away his position, Dave scanned the area behind them, shifting in a circle. Sliding back down into the gully, he went straight toward Rand.

"They aren't following. What do you want to do?"

Rand knew Cal and Jeb wouldn't be able to find the gang when they returned from Splendor. Retaliation against Banderas filled every thought, drove his actions. Until the deputy was dead, he wouldn't be able to put Hoot's murder behind him. Murder at the hand of a duly sworn lawman.

"We turn around."

"To where?"

"Splendor."

Shane walked beside Angela, wanting to hold her hand, settling for her arm through his. He would've considered it if Martha hadn't been joining them for supper. Funny how holding hands was seen as more intimate than one arm slipped through another. As long as Angela walked beside him, Shane didn't care.

"Did you arrest anyone today, Deputy?" Martha fought addressing him by his first name.

"We arrested one man, Miss van Plew."

"What did he do? Steal a loaf of bread or a can of corn?"

"He tried to kill me."

The women came to a stop, mouths open. "What?" Angela choked out.

"Came right behind me. Shouldn't have happened."

Tugging on his arm, Angela forced him to stop. "I want details, Shane."

"We have reservations at the Eagle's Nest. I'll explain and answer all your questions after we're seated." She didn't want to wait. Shane didn't want to talk about it on the boardwalk, where others could hear.

"He's right, Angela. It will be much nicer to hear the details at our own table. Not out in the open." Martha's reasonable response won out.

The table Shane requested was perfect for a private conversation. Taking their seats, he ordered wine as their waiter handed out menus.

Martha's eyes lit in anticipation. "Such a wonderful selection. What do you suggest, Deputy?"

Grinning at her continued use of his title rather than his name, he lowered his menu. "Everything they serve is excellent. You'll want to order one of May's desserts."

"May?" Angela asked.

"The wife of Caleb Covington, another deputy. She's the pastry chef for the restaurant."

"Ah." Feeling her face flush, Angela glanced away. It would take time to accept Shane wanted her and no other woman.

The waiter stopped at their table. "Are you ready to order?" He looked to Martha first.

"The venison steak with gravy, please."

He shifted his attention to Angela. "Ma'am?"

"I'll have the veal with mushrooms, please."

"Deputy?"

"The roast duck with orange sauce."

"All your choices come with wild rice and mushrooms."

"That would be fine," Shane answered for all of them.

Angela hummed with impatience. "All right. Tell us about the man who tried to kill you."

He reminded her of his trip to Big Pine to bring back Harley Sloan. "We were trying to get him away from his father. Dale Sloan found out about it, and that I was the deputy who brought him here. He came after me. Another deputy, Cole Santori, saw what was happening and shot him."

Martha gasped. "Is he dead?"

"No, although it wouldn't be much of a loss. Sloan will be a visitor at the clinic for a couple more days."

Angela leaned toward him. "Why?"

"Sloan is a mean drunk. Beat up his wife, threatened his boys. He spent a year at Deer Lodge, a prison north of here. Sloan thought he could force me to tell him where Harley is holed up. Instead, he'll probably be sent back to Deer Lodge. For more than a year this time."

Except for comments about the delicious food, they ate their meals in silence. Dessert was praised, the women saying how they couldn't eat another bite.

On the walk back, Shane threaded his fingers through hers, uncaring if someone disapproved. Martha went into the house ahead of them, leaving Angela and Shane time to talk.

"I had a wonderful time, Shane. Thank you."

Cupping her face in his hands, he brushed a kiss over her lips before stepping away.

Gripping his arms, she kissed him again. "I'm not ready for the night to end."

Moving a few errant strands of hair off her face, he couldn't look away. "Ride with me to the cabin."

"Yes."

"I have tomorrow off. I'll have Suzanne make food to take with us."

Caressing his face, odd sensations fluttered in her stomach. "I'll do it."

"All right. I'll have the horses ready at nine."

"Perfect."

"We'll be gone all day."

Angela smiled up at him. "Sounds wonderful."

Kissing her once more, he took her hand, leading her up the steps to her door. Without another word, he waited until she walked inside, closing the door behind her.

Shane couldn't remember a time anything had felt so right. Not even when they were younger. Bounding down the steps, he closed the distance to his house, his thoughts on the day ahead. Not the hours keeping watch from the top floor of Ruby's Palace through the night.

Rand stood in the shadows, watching the couple. He'd left two men at the boardinghouse down the street, the rest in a new camp not far from town. Not that anyone would be expecting Sutton and his gang in Splendor. It would make killing the deputy even more satisfying.

Nothing would bring Hoot back. Nor fill the void in Rand's chest whenever he thought of his best friend.

The outlaw still couldn't believe his good fortune. From a chair near the window of Finn's, he'd watched, knowing the odds were small he'd spot Banderas. Downing two beers, he'd ordered a third when two ladies and a man walked toward the saloon.

He didn't recognize the deputy right away. When they stopped in front of Finn's, Sutton took a better look, almost falling out of his chair when he spotted the object of his rage.

Keeping his distance, Rand had followed them on their winding walk toward the east side of town. Hiding in the shadows between two houses, he watched and listened to Banderas and the woman.

His patience had been rewarded when the deputy invited her to join him at his cabin. The two of them away from town for most of the day. Plenty of time to kill Banderas and take the woman.

They'd be leaving at nine in the morning. He figured it wouldn't be hard to follow them, take them by surprise. Rand would take one of his men with him. Sutton would kill the deputy while his man took care of the woman. It would be over in minutes.

He hadn't planned a quick kill. Instead of minutes, he preferred Banderas die slowly, one bullet at a time. Maybe he'd make the woman watch.

Sutton hadn't felt so good in a long time. Since before Hoot died. His plans were coming together better than he'd hoped. By this time tomorrow, he'd have his revenge.

Chapter Twenty-Four

Gabe, Nick, Hawke, and Cole stood around the desk in the jail, studying the plans for the new saloon in Big Pine. The first two would be the owners. The others interested observers.

Hawke and Cole had come by after their shift watching the trails toward Big Pine. During the vigils the last few weeks, no one had seen a single sign the Sutton gang was anywhere near Splendor.

Cole's fingers traced the placement of the bar, tables, and piano. "When do you plan to open the saloon?"

"Within the month," Nick answered. "Some of the work has been done. We're waiting for the bar to be installed. Paul's moving over there in two weeks to hire the servers."

"Women, I hope," Cole joked, causing the others to laugh.

"It'll be run much like the Dixie." Gabe looked at Nick. "What did you learn about the gaming tables?"

"The roulette table and faro boards will arrive from Denver next week. We'll offer craps and card games, of course." Nick pulled out a cigar, holding it between his teeth. "I'm sure Gabe will make sure you boys try it all out."

Rolling up the drawing, Gabe put it aside. "Did either of you talk with Shane this morning?"

Hawke nodded. "He's taking Miss Baldwin to his cabin today."

Cole leaned against the desk, trying not to sound too interested. "What about Miss van Plew?"

Hawke shrugged. "I didn't ask."

"Maybe I'll pay a visit." Cole touched the brim of his hat. "Gentlemen."

―――

Shane paced around his house, wishing he'd told Angela they'd leave at eight instead of nine. After his uneventful shift on the top floor of Ruby's, he'd expected to fall into bed and sleep. It hadn't happened. Staring at the ceiling for an hour, he'd given up and made coffee, consuming the entire pot.

The sun had been up for over an hour, signaling the livery would be open. Strapping on his gunbelt, he snagged his hat from a table. Noah didn't do the blacksmithing any longer. The younger man he'd hired before Shane came to Splendor completed the physically demanding job, and managed the livery, while Noah took care of the saddlery shop.

Both men were present when Shane arrived. The livery was home to his pinto stallion, Onacona.

"Morning, Shane. You riding to the cabin this morning?" Noah took a measurement, glancing down at a stack of lumber. His plan to enlarge the livery had moved from an idea to ready to start.

He glanced away, recalling the last time Noah had seen him with Angela. "Miss Baldwin is riding with me. I'll need a horse for her."

Staring at him, Noah barked out a laugh. "Thought you didn't like the woman."

"We get along fine. Do you have a horse for me?"

Slapping Shane's back, Noah moved past him toward a stall housing a young, gentle mare. "This is Poppy. She's five. Bought her a year ago from the Pelletiers." Opening the gate, he stepped aside for Shane to walk in.

"Travis and Billy trained her?" He ran a hand along the palomino's shoulder, back, and flank.

"Dax told me Selina helped them out."

Selina had married Bram MacLaren in a quiet ceremony attended by his relatives from California and her family at Redemption's Edge. Noah, his wife, Abby, and a handful of townsfolk were also invited. They now lived at the MacLaren ranch east of Splendor.

Shane turned to face him. "We're leaving at nine. Show me the saddle and tack, and I'll get the mare and my horse ready." He glanced at the stack of wood. "You have enough to do."

"I'm never too busy to help a friend. I'll get Poppy tacked up while you ready your stallion. It'll give me something to do until the men arrive to enlarge the livery."

Noah walked to a storeroom, returning with a saddle and tack for the mare. "Have you heard any more about Sutton coming this way?"

Tossing the brush used to groom into a bucket, Shane's mouth twisted in disgust. "Nothing from Sheriff Sterling, or anyone else. You already know we have men watching the trails." He shook his head. "Sutton could be in the Dakotas by now."

"You don't believe he's waiting for the right time to strike?" Noah completed grooming Poppy, placing a blanket on her back before swinging the saddle on top.

"It's possible. Sutton doesn't have much patience. I would've expected him to come after me by now." Leading Onacona from the stall, Shane tossed the reins over a rail near the gate. Noah did the same with Poppy.

"We shouldn't stop watching for him."

Shane leaned his shoulder against the gate. "What are you saying?"

"You don't know the men in his gang. He could've sent a couple ahead to confirm you're here. Didn't you kill his closest friend when Sutton was arrested?"

"Can't swear to it, but he believes I did."

Noah rubbed his stubbled jaw, inclining his head. "He's a ruthless murderer. It's what he knows, what he understands."

"An eye for an eye?"

"People like Sutton don't give up when seeking vengeance, Shane. They wait for the right moment, and strike."

"Good morning, Shane." Angela swung the door wide. "Please, come in. I'm wrapping the last of the food."

"Hello, Deputy." Martha turned from her spot in the kitchen.

"Miss van Plew."

"Angela tells me you're riding to the cabin."

Shane took a step closer. "You're welcome to come with us."

"Thank you, but I have plans."

Angela finished putting the food into a burlap sack, closing it with a length of leather. "What plans?"

Shrugging, Martha held the sack still while Angela tightened the thong. "I met Ruth Paige yesterday. She invited me to join the meeting of the church women. It's held at noon, which means everyone brings something to share."

Angela lifted a brow. "Food?"

Crossing her arms, Martha's lips tipped into a grin. "You don't have to look so surprised. I'm going to purchase a cake from May Covington."

"Excellent idea." Picking up the sack, Angela met Shane in the living room. "I'm ready." Handing him the food, she retrieved her coat and reticule.

"Doubt you'll need the purse."

"Would you leave town without your gun?"

"It's not the same. I use the gun for protection. The reticule is for, well...I'm not certain what it's for." Placing his hand on the small of her back, he guided her to the door. "Last chance to come with us," he called over his shoulder.

Martha responded with a grin and wave.

Outside, Shane came to a halt when he spotted Cole at the base of the steps. "Tell me Gabe didn't send you to get me."

Cole's grin stretched from ear to ear. "I heard you were riding up to your cabin with Miss Baldwin."

"And?"

"Thought I'd come by to see if Miss van Plew would allow me to take her to lunch."

Angela's eyes widened. "Well, um, Deputy..."

Removing his hat, Cole gave a slight blow. "Deputy Santori, ma'am."

The front door opened, Martha looking down at them. "I thought you'd left."

"Martha, Deputy Santori has come by to ask you to lunch."

Passing Shane and Angela on the steps, he stopped in front of Martha. "Miss van Plew."

"Deputy Santori."

Grabbing Angela's hand, Shane grinned at her bewildered expression before walking the short distance to the livery.

"It's beautiful, Shane." Angela spoke about the ride up the hill. Most trees were still full of leaves, some losing their foliage early. They rode next to each other, her falling back when the trail narrowed. Not a half hour had passed since leaving the livery, yet she already noticed a change in the types of plants.

"How do you get a wagon up here? I mean, it would be hard to carry enough supplies for more than a day or two."

Shane pointed to their right. "There's another trail a little south of us. It's wider. A wagon will fit, but it takes twice as long to reach the cabin."

"Have you used it?"

"Not yet. Noah told me about it. He moved lumber, doors, windows, and furniture. I bought all the contents, as well as the cabin. You'll see it soon. We're almost there."

Shane wondered what he'd do if she didn't like it. The cabin, or the distance a half hour from town. He'd already put a good deal of work and all his money into the purchase, had planned to give up his house in town within the week. Rounding the last twist in the trail, he found himself holding his breath.

"Oh my, Shane. It's wonderful." Angela urged the mare forward, reining to a stop by the front porch. Not waiting for Shane, she slid to the ground and bounded up the steps. Turning in a circle, a broad smile lit her face. "When are you moving in?"

Relief flooded him. He couldn't have imagined her excitement at his new home. "Soon." Joining her on the porch, he unlocked the door, shoving it open. Taking her hand, he drew Angela inside. At mid-morning, there was plenty of light streaming from outside to see the interior.

Dropping his hand, she walked around the living room, fingers brushing over the furniture. "It's beautiful, Shane. May I?" She waved her hands toward the other rooms.

"Go ahead." Releasing the breath he'd been holding, he followed her. "It's not large. Noah laid it out to add more rooms."

Entering the bedroom, she stopped to take it all in. "Noah brought all this up here?"

"Yes. I bought the blanket at the Emporium. It will take time, Angie, but over time, I'll make the place mine." *Ours*, he hoped.

He knew her. Already sensed her mind considering on how to cozy it up. A woman's thing, he supposed. Warmth shot through him at the enthusiasm on her face.

Slipping past him, she took a quick glance into the indoor water closet before moving to the kitchen. Approaching the counter, she ran her hand along the woodwork.

"Did Noah make the cabinetry?"

"All of it. He put a great deal of time into creating the perfect home."

Turning, her gaze locked with his. "Why would he sell it?"

Chuckling, he hooked his thumbs inside the waistband of his pants. "The girl of his dreams agreed to marry him. Noah built a home for them on a hill above Splendor."

She stepped to him, wrapping her arms around his waist. "Perhaps this cabin will offer the same good luck for us, Shane."

Encircling her in his arms, he held her close. "Perhaps it will."

Chapter Twenty-Five

Rand followed the trail, keeping a good distance behind them. Far enough so his horse couldn't be heard. Alongside him rode another member of the gang, and one of their best shots. Dave knew what would be expected of him, assuring Rand he had no issue abducting a woman. Sutton wasn't surprised. There wasn't much the man wouldn't do.

If he and Hoot had been taking this trail, they may have stopped to enjoy the seclusion. Hoot might've been a big, brawny man, but he had a softer side. He refused to harm animals and children. Found joy in sunrises and sunsets.

Not a talkative man, Hoot could go on for an hour about a rainbow or double waterfall. Rand still found it hard to believe the man was gone. His rage returned. Banderas didn't deserve to walk around, breathe, sleep, and have a woman when Hoot would never experience any of those again.

It hadn't been hard getting information on the cabin. Most everyone in town knew Noah Brandt, and the small home he'd built not far up the mountain.

Resting his hand on the butt of his revolver, Rand played the scenario they'd agreed upon in his head. They'd wait until Banderas and his woman were inside the cabin. Dave would go in the front door. He'd go in the back. Surprise would do much of the work for them.

Hearing horses up ahead, Rand slowed, as did Dave. Instinct told him they'd reached the cabin. Dismounting, they led their mounts off the trail, far enough so they couldn't be spotted. Taking their time, the men made their way forward, stopping about fifty yards away, where two horses grazed.

They had a good view of the barn, a corral, and the front of the cabin. From their position, Rand was certain Banderas wouldn't be able to see them. He had to admit the man had purchased a real nice place. A place Rand might enjoy for a few days before gathering his men to ride east.

The front door opened, the woman stepping onto the porch ahead of the deputy. She rested her hands on the rail, looking toward the barn. The sight of the man who'd murdered Hoot sliced through him.

It would be easy to draw his gun, shoot Banderas and the woman from where he hid. What he craved would be over in a matter of seconds. Too quick for what he had planned.

Slipping his arm around the woman's waist, the deputy kissed her before guiding her down the steps toward the barn. Rand resisted the urge to change his plans, confront them there instead of inside the cabin.

It was times such as these when he wished he'd been born with more patience. He'd never been one to put off immediate pleasure. Rand had never seen the sense of it. Today might be the first time waiting would bring maximum gratification.

"It's larger than it appears from the outside." Angela repeated what she'd done in the cabin. Moving from one stall to the next, then opening the storeroom door to peer inside, she looked up to see a loft.

Without asking, she hurried to the ladder, climbing before Shane could stop her. Not that he would. He loved her enthusiasm, the genuine appreciation of all she'd seen.

"Have you been up here?" Angela called down.

"Not yet."

"Wonderful. Come join me and I'll share it with you."

An invitation he couldn't ignore. Chuckling, it took little time to reach the landing. What he saw surprised him. The loft was filled with crates holding tools, pots, pans, lanterns, and extra tack. He wondered if Noah remembered storing what amounted to over a hundred dollars worth of goods. Shane would have to ask him when they returned the horses.

Turning around, he saw Angela standing by an open door used for dropping hay to the ground. Crossing the short distance, he set his hands on her shoulders.

"There's still a lot of work to be done."

"Nothing we can't handle."

There it was again, the hint of a shared future. He and Angela had spoken this way, as if a life together was assured, more times than he could count. Years ago, when neither had expected to ever separate.

Wrapping his arms around her waist, he tugged her against his chest. "Do you think you could live in a place like this?"

Resting her head against his shoulder, she thought about the question. A half hour from town. No general store, meat market, or restaurants. No neighbors for miles. Not a soul to help if Shane was in town. She considered the animals Shane had told her about. Bears, wolves, and mountain lions.

"You'd have to teach me how to shoot a gun for when you aren't here."

Of all she could've said, that was the last thing he expected. Throwing back his head, he laughed.

"Are you certain about this, Jeb?"

"You've asked me the same question a hundred times already."

Cal shoved his hat from his forehead. "Making certain is all."

They crouched about thirty yards from the cabin, hidden from both the deputy and his hunters, keeping their voices to a whisper. Instinct, and something deep in Jeb's gut, told him to turn around when they'd almost reached Idaho. There were times those feelings meant nothing. Most often, he'd done well to heed them. Cal had learned not to argue when Jeb got the itch at the back of his neck.

"Sutton following them may mean nothing," Jeb said.

"Doesn't look that way to me." Cal scratched his jaw. "Rand wouldn't have ridden up this way unless this was where he planned to kill Banderas. We know he wants the woman. Doing it here will take care of both without witnesses."

Jeb and Cal had entered the edges of Splendor that morning, seeing Banderas and Miss Baldwin leaving the livery. A few minutes later, Rand and Dave showed up, heading in the same direction. They'd followed their former boss not long afterward.

"Can't let them do that, Cal."

Of all they'd done, the two refused to hurt women or children. If Rand had intended to rob the bank and kill the deputy, they might've gone along—as long as Sutton was the one to pull the trigger. What they saw in front of them made their stomachs turn.

"You're right." Shifting to relieve his tight muscles, Cal's gazed narrowed. "He'll wait until they're back in the cabin. Dave will go in the front. Rand the back." He glanced at Jeb. "He always takes the safer position. While Dave grabs Miss Baldwin, Rand will kill the deputy."

"And make her watch."

"They'll take her with them, dump her along the trail when Rand and the others have had their fill." Jeb picked up the rifle on the ground next to him.

"You gonna use that or your six-shooter?"

"Don't know. I'll make up my mind when Rand makes his move."

Cal looked down at his own rifle, glad he'd carried it from where they'd left their horses. He was good with a revolver, but a dead shot with a rifle.

Reaching into a pocket, Jeb retrieved a strip of jerky, tearing off a bite. "You sure you want to go to Idaho. Maybe Utah would be better."

Shoulders relaxing, Cal chewed his own jerky, his gaze shifting between the barn and cabin. "I don't care, as long as it's a long way from the Montana Territory. Can't go back to Wyoming. Colorado wouldn't be safe, either. Texas Rangers are already looking for us. Maybe California? Arizona?"

"Never been to either one," Jeb answered.

"California. I hear there's a lot of work."

"San Francisco's supposed to be a sight to see. Let's start there." Mouth dry, Cal wished he'd brought his canteen.

"San Francisco it is. Wonder when they'll leave the barn?"

"You anxious to get this over with?"

Jeb cocked a brow. "Aren't you?"

"All I want is to make sure Miss Baldwin is safe and get out of Montana. Can't come soon enough for me."

"We can't let anyone see us, Cal. We kill Rand and Dave, then ride out before the deputy gets a good look at us."

"No look at all would suit me," Cal added. "Leave the bodies?"

"Let Banderas explain the deaths to the sheriff."

"Miss Baldwin will back up his story." Cal got to his knees. "They're coming out of the barn. Heading straight for the cabin."

Jeb's gaze shifted to where Rand and Dave hunkered down, unaware they were being watched. Both men drew up, spotting the couple leaving the barn. "Sutton just saw them."

Cal swallowed the last of his jerky, picked up his rifle, and waited.

Banderas, his hand in Angela's, veered away from the cabin, walking straight for the creek about fifty feet away. "If there's an extra bad winter, such as we had this year, Noah said there's a chance of the creek overflowing. It's why he built the cabin a little higher off the ground."

"What happened last winter?"

"A blizzard in December was followed by a series of storms, each one bigger than the last. When spring came, all the creeks, lakes, and rivers overflowed. Noah told me the water came to within a few feet of the cabin. He and a couple men filled buckets, dumping the water into the barrels. It's the end of summer and most of the barrels are still full."

Stopping at the edge of the creek, he motioned around them. "Lots of deer and elk. Plenty of fish. In the spring and summer, the bushes are filled with berries."

Angela nodded behind them. "I saw the large stack of firewood."

"I've added to what Noah started. There will be more chores during winter." Shane's voice lowered. "Living out here isn't easy, Angie."

Crossing her arms, she glared up at him. "Are you trying to convince me I don't have the grit for this kind of life?"

The anger in her voice told him much about what she could endure. He ran the back of his knuckles down her cheek. "What do you believe?"

Dropping her arms, she caught the scent of the fire he'd built in one of the stoves before they left for the barn. It comforted her in an unexplainable way.

"There's no way to be sure until I've spent time up here, Shane. We both know marriage would come first. As much as I believe my future lies with you, I can tell you aren't convinced. Trust is still an issue. You need more time, whereas, I do not."

Shane studied her, unsure of what she was telling him. There were no tears lingering behind her eyes, nothing in her voice to signal she would no longer wait.

"I love you, Angie."

"Yes, I know. I'll wait, but not forever." She started to turn back toward the cabin, then stopped. "You'll never find a woman who loves you as much as me. One who is as committed to a life together." She tapped a hand over her heart. "You don't yet believe it here, where it counts."

Moving her hand to her forehead, she tapped again. "And you aren't ready to trust me here."

Shane's heart stuttered, stomach clenching, as he watched her leave him alone at the creek. Angela hadn't given him an ultimatum, for which he was grateful.

She'd called him on his doubts. Uncertainties from his past, distrust of the future. Hawke would clasp his shoulder, encourage him not to lose Angela a second time. Take the chance and expect the best, the same as Hawke had done with Beauty.

Taking one step, then another, he followed her back to the cabin. Shane prayed his hesitation hadn't ruined the progress they'd made.

Hadn't damaged her belief in a future together.

Chapter Twenty-Six

Stepping inside, Shane hesitated. Angela smiled at him while setting out food on the table meant for four. His mouth watered as she continued to remove wrappings from all she'd made.

"Fried chicken, canned peaches, boiled eggs, biscuits with jam, and apple fritters." She surveyed their meal, brushing both hands down an apron she'd found on a hook in the kitchen. "Is there enough?"

Blowing out a chuckle, he joined her at the table. "Plenty. You did all this last night?"

"I boiled the eggs and made the fritters before going to bed. The rest I fixed this morning. Are there plates and utensils?"

"In the kitchen. I'll get them." Walking out of her view, he set fisted hands on his hips, staring up at the closed cabinet. He was a fool. He'd be a bigger one if he let Angela get away.

Pulling down the plates and gathering utensils, Shane would wait to ask her to marry him until after their meal. He pictured them walking back to the creek, him dropping to one knee. Waiting a moment, he didn't experience the fear expected. A grin tipped the corners of his mouth. This was right. Always had been.

"Here you go." Setting them on the table, he couldn't help staring at her. Still no apprehension.

"Are you all right, Shane?"

Giving a quick shake of his head, he pulled out her chair. "I'm fine, Angie. Just hungry."

Her smile slammed into his gut. How had he ever thought he could go through life without her brilliant smile?

Filling their plates, he dug right in while she picked at a piece of chicken. Shane ignored the urge to set down his biscuit and ask her right there. She deserved better than a hasty proposal. Angela deserved for him to do it right, within sight of the creek she found so beautiful.

***

"It's time." Rand rose until he bent at the waist, drawing his gun. "You go in the front."

"We've been over this, boss," Dave groused, checking the chambers of the six-shooter once more. "How hard can it be to restrain one woman while you finish off Banderas?"

"You don't know the deputy. Don't underestimate him." Waving his gun toward the barn, Rand signaled Dave to move.

Watching his man cover the distance to take a position inside the barn, Sutton glanced around. The air had gone still. If Banderas was outside, he'd notice the quiet, be on alert. A sneer twisted the outlaw's mouth. He could almost taste victory over the deputy who'd killed Hoot.

Sending a curt nod at Dave, Rand turned to his right, his steps slow and careful as he covered the distance to the back door. Rushing the last few yards, he rested his back against the cabin, letting out a relieved breath. He hadn't been spotted.

Laughter came from inside the cabin, making his blood turn cold. The higher pitch of the woman, mixed with the deep chuckles from the deputy, served to ignite Rand's rage. Why were they enjoying life while Hoot rotted in a pauper's grave near Cheyenne?

Moving to the corner of the cabin, he spotted Dave in the barn, his gun raised as he waited for his boss's sign. Tilting his head back, Rand looked at the sky. He wasn't a praying man, never spoke to God, and didn't intend to start now. His future had been guaranteed years ago, and it wasn't going to end in heaven.

Touching the brim of his hat, Sutton gave the sign for Dave to move. Staying low, he ran toward the cabin, dropping to a knee at the bottom of the steps. The next part would be the hardest. Getting to the front door without Banderas hearing his footfalls.

Careful, so as not to alert those inside, Dave took one step, then another, holding his breath. He knew Rand couldn't see him. His boss's signal to enter through the back would be the sound of the front door crashing open.

Reaching the door, Dave swiped an arm across his forehead. Hearing voices, he breathed a sigh of relief. They hadn't heard him. Had no idea their peaceful existence was about to end.

Raising his gun, Dave turned, raised one booted foot, and kicked in the door.

Jeb and Cal had watched Rand and Dave make their move. Given the clear sky and bright sun, the plan was bold. Their former boss rested his back against the back of the cabin. Dave did the same in the front. The men were within seconds from going after their prey.

"You ready, Cal?" Jeb gripped the rifle at his side, ready to put an end to Rand's revenge.

Cal didn't shift his attention from the cabin. "Who do you want?"

"Rand."

"I've got Dave. Put a bullet in Rand for me."

Jeb didn't respond. He planned to bury more than two bullets into the man. If their plan worked, he'd empty his six-shooter into the man without a flicker of guilt.

The instant Dave raised his boot, kicking open the door, the waiting was over. Moving through the cover of the brush, both men rushed toward the cabin. Cal toward the front, Jeb toward the back.

Consumed with their revenge, neither Rand nor Dave noticed them hurrying to the cabin. Weren't prepared for the end rushing toward them.

Shane jumped at the front door crashing open, his chair hitting the floor behind him. He reached for his six-shooter, remembering he'd removed his gunbelt, his weapon now feet away.

He didn't recognize the man holding his weapon on Angela. Acting on instinct, he shoved her aside, rushing their assailant. Hearing the sound of a discharging gun, he was surprised at the lack of pain. The man didn't have the best aim.

"Get down, Angie!"

Grabbing the intruder's foot, he twisted hard, hearing the man curse at the time the back door burst open. A quick glance had his chest bursting.

Rand Sutton stalked inside, his gun aimed at Angela. Shane's grip on the other man didn't change.

"What do you want, Sutton?"

Barking out a laugh, he fired, landing a bullet within inches of Angela's head. He laughed again at her scream. Shane dropped his hold on the other man, moving toward her. Rand fired again. The bullet slammed into the floor next to Shane's shoulder.

"Try that again, and this will be over much too soon. You all right, Dave?"

"Why are you here?" Shane flashed a glance at his gun two feet away.

"You're a bright guy, Banderas. Why do you think I'm here?"

"Angela isn't a part of this. Let her go. Do what you want with me."

"She stays. Have no doubt I'm going to do what I've intended since Hoot died. Tie up the woman, Dave."

Angela's eyes flashed with anger when Dave reached for her. "Don't touch me, you...miscreant." She tried to scoot away, hitting the edge of the sofa.

"Miscreant?" Dave chuckled, pulling leather thongs from a pocket. "Don't know that anyone's ever called me that."

"It's not a compliment," Angela spit out.

Rand moved closer to Shane, the gun aimed at his head. "Don't try to stop him, Banderas. I'll have to shoot you if you do."

Meeting her gaze, Shane mouthed the words, *I'm sorry*, before looking back up at Rand. "She doesn't need to watch what you have planned." He'd been inching toward his gun. There was little chance he could hit more than one. He'd make certain it was Rand.

Grabbing Angela's wrists, Dave yanked them behind her, eliciting a scream of pain.

"You're a horrible person," she bit out, wincing as he tightened the thongs.

Dave chuckled. "Is that better than a miscreant?"

She didn't answer. Focusing on Shane, Angela tried to draw strength from him. They wouldn't die like this. Not when they'd found each other after all these years.

The air whooshed from her when Dave dragged her up, shoving her into a chair. "This where you want her, boss?"

"Good as any." An unsettling gleam shown in Rand's eyes.

Shane had no doubt what the outlaw planned. His mind whirled. He couldn't allow Angela to witness his death. The sight of his blood, his still body, would stay with her for years.

"Take her outside." Shane's voice was an order, rigid and unwavering.

"You're not in a position to bargain, Deputy. Or have you forgotten who holds the gun."

"Move her back a little, Dave." Rand stared at her. "Don't want her pretty face splattered with blood."

The sound of her chair scraping against the floor sounded Shane's death knoll. He knew it wouldn't be long now. If he made a move, he had seconds to act.

Everything happened at once.

Shane lunged for his revolver as Rand aimed for his chest. Angela screamed, shoving her chair backward, ramming it into the stomach of an unsuspecting Dave. Losing his balance, he reached for the back of the chair, pushing it sideways.

A shot rang out, then another. Shane stared in shock. He hadn't fired his gun. Rand dropped to his knees, clutching his chest as blood trickled from the corners of his mouth.

Across the room, Dave's lifeless eyes stared straight ahead, a bullet hole in the center of his forehead. Shane's jawed dropped open. He had not fired his weapon.

Jumping up, holding his gun in front of him, Shane looked into the kitchen. Nothing. He shifted to the bedroom. Again, he saw nothing. The front door still stood open. Rushing outside, he scanned the area. He stood still, listening. Then he heard it.

Horses pounding along the trail, heading away from the cabin.

Chapter Twenty-Seven

Releasing the thongs binding her to the chair, Shane wrapped his arms around Angela. "Are you all right?"

She clung to him, her head against his shoulder. "Other than my back, head, and hip, I believe I'm going to live."

He would've laughed at her bravado. Cupping Angela's face with his hands, he brushed a kiss across her lips before lifting her into his arms. Striding into the bedroom, he laid her in the center of the bed, checking for blood.

"I wasn't hit, Shane. Dave slammed me to the floor. I'm bruised, nothing more."

Grabbing a towel, he dabbed at the corners of her eyes, then her mouth. "Blood." Shane's anger returned. He wished Rand and Dave were still alive so he could kill them himself.

"Pretty feisty for someone who almost died."

She stroked his cheek, eyes locking on his. "You were the one they wanted."

Shane wouldn't voice his fear when they tied her to the chair. That's when their plan became clear. Rand would've taken her with them, used her, then handed her off to the rest of the gang. When they were done, her body would have been buried in a shallow grave off whatever trail they rode.

Running a hand over her hair, he rested his forehead against hers. "Yes, I was. And now they're dead. They won't hurt anyone else."

"I'm still hungry."

Shaking his head, he laughed, unable to contain his relief any longer. He thought of the bodies, the blood, all he'd have to do for the cabin to return to normal.

"Did you kill them?"

"No."

Her eyes widened. "Then, who did?"

"I don't know." He'd tell Gabe about hearing horses riding away. Not one. Two, perhaps. "Right now, I don't care. We're alive, Angie. That's enough for now."

Splendor

Angela had argued, threatened, said she'd salt all his food, but Shane took her straight to the clinic. Doc Worthington, along with his nurse, Carrie, checked her over, giving Angela a small tin of salve for the bruises.

"She's lucky, Shane." Carrie touched his arm. "It's her, isn't it?" She smiled up at him, no condemnation in her eyes or voice. He still believed she was one of the best women he'd ever known. Shane lowered himself into a chair in the front room, motioning her to sit next to him.

"Yes. Angela Baldwin." Clasping his hands together, he leaned forward. "I've loved her my entire life." Shane didn't say more. The rest was between him and Angela.

"She's a very lucky woman."

The front door opened. Griffin MacKenzie entered, walking straight toward them. A good friend of Bram and Thane MacLaren, he'd accepted a partnership in Francesca Boudreaux's law firm. She and Zeke, a fellow deputy, had married a year ago. He didn't miss how MacKenzie's gaze kept moving toward Carrie.

Shane stood, extending his hand. "Griff."

"Shane. Miss Galloway."

"Hello, Mr. MacKenzie. What brings you into the clinic?"

"I have a meeting with Doc Worthington about some property he wants to buy. Is he still here?"

Shane jumped up when the door to the exam room opened. Angela stood in the opening. Settling an arm over her shoulders, he guided her toward Carrie and Griffin.

"How are you feeling?"

"A small headache is all." Angela held out the tin. "Salve for the cuts and bruises." Her gaze darted to Carrie. "Thank you for helping me."

"Of course. Have you met Griff MacKenzie? He's one of the attorneys in town." Carrie smiled up at him. "One of two. Griff, this is Angela Baldwin. She's new to Splendor."

Angela thought of her inheritance, and how she'd need someone such as MacKenzie if she stayed in Splendor.

"It's a pleasure, ma'am. You appear to have had a run-in with something."

Shane answered for her. "Rand Sutton and one of his men followed us to the cabin."

Griffin's face clouded. "I assume they're dead." Few people knew about his past as a gunslinger. Gabe and the deputies were some, as well as the Pelletiers. He was a good man to know.

"Yes, but not from my hand."

Griffin's brows drew together. "Perhaps we can talk tomorrow."

"I'll come to your office."

"Griff." Doc Worthington left the exam room, shaking the lawyer's hand. "Let's go upstairs to my office. My wife will be joining us soon."

Shane didn't miss the way Carrie's attention stayed with Griffin as he climbed the stairs, or the way he glanced over his shoulder at her. He grinned, reminding himself how life had a way of working out.

"I need to clean the exam room. Hope you're feeling better soon, Miss Baldwin."

"Please call me Angela."

"Then you must call me Carrie."

Shane waited until the exam door closed before placing his hand at the small of Angela's back. "Are you still hungry?"

"Famished." She touched her hair. "I'll scare the patrons if we go to a restaurant.'

"That's not possible, Angie. You're always beautiful."

Her laughing eyes said she didn't quite believe him.

"You have a small cut at the corner of one eye, and a little bruising on your cheek. If we go to McCall's, Betts will get us a table near the kitchen. Take a chance, sweetheart."

Angela thought about how much she loved him before nodding. It was not quite five when they entered McCall's. Two tables were empty. One in the middle of the room, and the other by the kitchen door. No one ever wanted to sit there. This evening, Shane led her to the back.

Betts walked toward them, a cup of coffee in one hand. "You know there's a table up front, Deputy."

Shane pulled out a chair for Angela. "This will be fine, Betts."

"I'll get cups for you."

When Betts returned, each ordered the special. They spoke little, lost in their own thoughts. Angela wondering where they'd go from here. Shane knowing, searching for the right words.

His vision of dropping to one knee by the creek was shattered by the actions of the day. Massaging the back of his neck, an idea struck him. A slow grin stretched across his face.

"Would you walk with me a bit before I escort you home?"

Angela felt another wave of exhaustion. She wanted a bath and to climb under her covers. "That would be nice."

Taking her hand, he headed toward the school, and Noah's bench. As they walked, he felt her gaze on him. He knew she was tired, but this couldn't wait. After today, he didn't want her changing her mind about living in Splendor, in the cabin with him.

Reaching the bench, they sat. Shane didn't let go of her hand, and she didn't pull away. Listening to the water, a peace washed through him.

Before he had a chance to second-guess himself or lose his courage, he shifted, dropping to one knee. Taking both her hands, he looked up to see shock and moisture in both eyes.

"I love you, Angie. Always have, and that will never change. We've both made mistakes. You're still the only woman I want to share my life. No one else." His heart slammed against his chest when her tears spilled onto her cheek. "Marry me, Angie. Share my cabin in the woods. Have children..." He didn't finish as she launched forward, wrapping her arms around his neck. Gripping her around the waist, he laughed. "Is that a yes?"

Swiping tears from her face, she nodded. "Yes...yes...yes. Always and forever."

Epilogue

Three weeks later...

Martha stood close to the woman who'd become her closest friend, watching as Angela and Shane took their vows. Happy they'd found each other again, she still battled a pang of unease since the morning they'd announced their plans.

Reverend Paige said Shane could kiss his bride, which he did with exuberance to the cheers of those in attendance. Facing their friends, Martha's stomach clenched at their broad smiles. She'd never seen two people so in love, so happy.

Staying behind as the couple made their way through the well-wishers, she was tempted to go home instead of staying for refreshments. The idea was short-lived. Martha wouldn't do anything to upset Angela on her wedding day.

"Good afternoon, Miss van Plew." Cole had removed his hat, his warm smile drifting through her.

They had a wonderful time the day Shane and Angela rode to his cabin. She'd attended the meeting of the church women, then Cole returned. They'd taken a ride toward the Pelletier ranch, turning around before she could see the large house she'd heard so much about. An early supper at the boardinghouse had ended their day. She hadn't heard from him since.

"Mr. Santori." Keeping her tone neutral, Martha looked over the crowd. Some were already walking through the back door to the community building behind the church.

"May I escort you to the reception?"

Meeting his expectant gaze, she gave a slight nod. "That would be wonderful."

Slipping her arm through his, they made the short trip into the large space, now filled with people who'd chosen to spend a Sunday afternoon with a couple most barely knew. Martha wanted friends such as these.

Across the room, Griffin MacKenzie stood with several men, holding a glass of punch. Noticing Cole, he gave a slight nod before turning his ear back to the conversation in the group. He'd heard the story several times. The way mystery gunslingers killed Sutton and one of his men, then rode off, saving Shane and Angela. It was a good story, with an even better ending. Shane asked Angela to marry him that same night.

Griffin intended to find a certain woman who'd attended the ceremony. Then he spotted her. Carrie Galloway laughed at something one of the women around her said. He recognized them, but his attention stayed on Carrie. Griffin had yet to find the courage to invite her to share a meal with him. He groaned at the thought. One slight woman scaring him more than the many gunslingers he'd put in the ground.

"Griff, what do you think?" Gabe had joined the group.

Taking a swallow of punch, he shook his head. "My mind was elsewhere."

"We were talking about the rustlers. They've struck the MacLarens, and three ranchers to the south. About thirty head total. The MacLarens can handle the loss, but it's too many for the smaller spreads."

"The thefts are south of town?" Griffin asked.

"Other than Bram's ranch, yes. I don't have enough men to help the ranchers keep watch. Those to the west and north know about the rustling, and are taking precautions."

"Not much more you can do, Gabe." Seeing Carrie watching the group from across the room, Griffin excused himself.

Before he could reach her, Dutch McFarlin stopped beside Carrie, handing out a glass of punch. The deputy kept a larger than appropriate distance between them, making Griffin wonder if Dutch had an interest in her more than as a friend.

Hesitating a moment too long, he felt a hand on his arm. Glancing down, he smiled at Rose Keenen.

"Hello, Rose." In the background, he heard the four piece band playing. Knowing she loved to dance, his thoughts of spending time with Carrie faded.

"Griff." When the band began a spirited tune, she inclined her head toward the tiny area reserved for dancing.

Chuckling, he took her hand. "Would you care to dance?"

"I'd love to."

Holding her in his arms while keeping up with the music, he wondered why Rose didn't stir his blood the same as Carrie. It would make his life easier if she did.

Swirling Rose around, his gaze lit on Carrie. Dutch no longer stood beside her. Griffin wished he hadn't been so hasty in asking Rose to dance. When the music ended, he'd excuse himself to find Carrie.

Escorting Rose off the dance floor, Griffin thanked her before turning toward where he'd last seen Carrie. She wasn't there. Crossing to the other side of the room, he stopped near the table holding the cake and numerous pies, not seeing her.

Out of the corner of his eye, he caught movement. A green dress, the same color as Carrie wore. Turning in her direction, his stomach wrenched into a knot.

She was headed out the door on the arm of Dutch McFarlin.

Thank you for taking the time to read Silent Sunset. If you enjoyed it, please consider telling your friends or posting a short review. Word of mouth is an author's best friend and much appreciated.

Watch for book twenty in the Redemption Mountain series, **Rocky Basin.**

If you want in on all the backstage action of my historical westerns, join my VIP Readers Group at:
https://geni.us/VIPReadersGroup

Join my Newsletter to be notified of Pre-Orders and New Releases:
https://www.shirleendavies.com/

I care about quality, so if you find an error, please contact me via email at
shirleen@shirleendavies.com

About the Author

Shirleen Davies writes romance. She is the best-selling author of books in the romantic suspense, military romance, historical western romance, and contemporary western romance genres. Shirleen grew up in Southern California, attended Oregon State University, and has degrees from San Diego State University and the University of Maryland. Her passion is writing emotionally charged stories of flawed people who find redemption through love and acceptance. She lives with her husband in a beautiful town in northern Arizona.

I love to hear from my readers!

Send me an email: shirleen@shirleendavies.com
Visit my Website: https://www.shirleendavies.com/
Sign up to be notified of New Releases:
https://www.shirleendavies.com/
Follow me on Amazon:
http://www.amazon.com/author/shirleendavies
Follow me on BookBub:
https://www.bookbub.com/authors/shirleen-davies

Other ways to connect with me:

Facebook Author Page: http://www.facebook.com/shirleendaviesauthor
Twitter: www.twitter.com/shirleendavies
Pinterest: http://pinterest.com/shirleendavies
Instagram: https://www.instagram.com/shirleendavies_author/

Books by Shirleen Davies

Historical Western Romance Series

Redemption Mountain

Redemption's Edge, Book One
Wildfire Creek, Book Two
Sunrise Ridge, Book Three
Dixie Moon, Book Four
Survivor Pass, Book Five
Promise Trail, Book Six
Deep River, Book Seven
Courage Canyon, Book Eight
Forsaken Falls, Book Nine
Solitude Gorge, Book Ten
Rogue Rapids, Book Eleven
Angel Peak, Book Twelve
Restless Wind, Book Thirteen
Storm Summit, Book Fourteen
Mystery Mesa, Book Fifteen
Thunder Valley, Book Sixteen
A Very Splendor Christmas, Holiday Novella, Book Seventeen
Paradise Point, Book Eighteen,
Silent Sunset, Book Nineteen
Rocky Basin, Book Twenty, Coming Next in the Series!

MacLarens of Boundary Mountain

Colin's Quest, Book One,

Brodie's Gamble, Book Two
Quinn's Honor, Book Three
Sam's Legacy, Book Four
Heather's Choice, Book Five
Nate's Destiny, Book Six
Blaine's Wager, Book Seven
Fletcher's Pride, Book Eight
Bay's Desire, Book Nine
Cam's Hope, Book Ten

MacLarens of Fire Mountain

Tougher than the Rest, Book One
Faster than the Rest, Book Two
Harder than the Rest, Book Three
Stronger than the Rest, Book Four
Deadlier than the Rest, Book Five
Wilder than the Rest, Book Six

Romantic Suspense

Eternal Brethren, Military Romantic Suspense

Steadfast, Book One
Shattered, Book Two
Haunted, Book Three
Untamed, Book Four
Devoted, Book Five
Faithful, Book Six
Exposed, Book Seven
Undaunted, Book Eight

Resolute, Book Nine
Unspoken, Book Ten
Defiant, Book Eleven, Coming Next in the Series!

Peregrine Bay, Romantic Suspense

Reclaiming Love, Book One
Our Kind of Love, Book Two
Edge of Love, Book Three, Coming Next in the Series!

Contemporary Romance Series

MacLarens of Fire Mountain

Second Summer, Book One
Hard Landing, Book Two
One More Day, Book Three
All Your Nights, Book Four
Always Love You, Book Five
Hearts Don't Lie, Book Six
No Getting Over You, Book Seven
'Til the Sun Comes Up, Book Eight
Foolish Heart, Book Nine

Macklin's of Burnt River

Thorn's Journey
Del's Choice
Boone's Surrender

The best way to stay in touch is to subscribe to my newsletter. Go to: https://www.shirleendavies.com/ and subscribe in the box at the top of the right column that asks for your email. You'll be notified of new books before they are released, have chances to win great prizes, and receive other subscriber-only specials.

Copyright © 2021 by Shirleen Davies

All rights reserved. No part of this publication may be reproduced, distributed, or transmitted in any form or by any electronic or mechanical means, including information storage and retrieval systems or transmitted in any form or by any means without the prior written permission of the publisher, except by a reviewer who may quote brief passages in a review. Thank you for respecting the hard work of this author.

For permission requests, contact the publisher.

Avalanche Ranch Press, LLC
PO Box 12618
Prescott, AZ 86304

Silent Sunset is a work of fiction. Names, characters, places, and incidents are either products of the author's imagination or used fictitiously. Any resemblance to actual events, locales, or persons, living or dead, is wholly coincidental.

Made in the USA
Middletown, DE
18 October 2022